THE JAIL DANCING

*and other Stories of
an Old Scottish Town*

THE SAGART

THE JAIL DANCING

and other Stories of an
Old Scottish Town

(Inverness)

BY EONA MACNICOL

Illustrated by John Mackay

ALBYN PRESS LTD
EDINBURGH

Photoset by
Specialised Offset Services Limited, Liverpool
Made and printed
in Great Britain by
The Garden City Press Ltd
Letchworth, Hertfordshire
and published by
ALBYN PRESS LTD
2 & 3 Abbeymount
Edinburgh

The publishers acknowledge the financial
assistance of the Scottish Arts Council
in the publication of this volume

CONTENTS

The first story is set in the seventeenth century, and most are of eighteenth-century period; with "The Absence of Mr Clark" we turn into the nineteenth century, and "Maggie the Shoppie" is early twentieth century.

To
the late Meg MacDougall
Librarian of Inverness
this book is dedicated in love and homage

ACKNOWLEDGEMENTS

I am grateful to the Editor of *Blackwood's Magazine* for permission to include in this volume "A Work of Necessity" and "The Little Shoemaker", and to the Editor of *The Scots Magazine* for permission to include "A Dark Grey Coat"; also to the BBC for "Maggie the Shoppie".

I should also like to thank Inverness Library, where I first found the sources of some of the stories, and the Scottish Room of the George IV Bridge Edinburgh Public Library where, more recently, I have been able to continue research.

Nor is it out of place to acknowledge my indebtedness to two gentlemen long dead, John Maclean and Charles Bond, whose *Reminiscences of a Clachnacuddin Nonagenarian* has provided me not only with sources but with many a smile!

PRINCIPAL SOURCES

I have followed, though not always closely, the following:

(1) Inverness Kirk Session Records; (2) John Maclean (ed. Bond) *Reminiscences of a Clachnacuddin Nonagenarian*; (3) RCN; (4) RCN, Memoirs of the Life of Duncan Forbes; (5) RCN, W. Mackay: *Urquhart and Glenmoriston*, various on the '45, especially Tayler; (6) RCN; (7) John Noble: *Miscellanea Invernessiana*; (8) RCN; (9) RCN; (10) RCN; (11) Extracts from *The Inverness Journal*, Shaw: *Digest of Decisions in the Supreme Court*, Lachlan Mackintosh of Raigmore: *Observations on … the Highlands of Scotland*.

Not the Righteous

AS THE BELL rang out slowly and more slowly, ready to be still, the elder stood in the doorway of the church, the latch in his hand. He heard the silence fall over the expectant people and scanned them with eagerness one by one: Duncan Rose the provost himself, and Stewart of Alvaig, and the captain of the garrison now in the town, and Forbes of Insh and his cousin, the dead earl's lady – they sat as doucely as the common folk. Aye, there was a goodly enough concourse; the place was filled for the most part, though here and there could be seen a shame of naked wood.

The elder saw the church officer come in and lay the Book down on the cushioned board, then turn himself reverently sideways to let the preacher pass. The preacher! The elder lifted his head and his breath came in audibly almost as if in pain: Robert his son, Robert his only begotten, new licensed, soon to be ordained. The elder gazed at the familiar head, seeing it with new eyes. He dared no longer consider that the brown hair was of the same shade and grew in the same manner as the dead mother's, nor that the brow and chin resembled his own. His love and pride were tempered with such awe. The people too seemed awed, for all the young man was familiar to them, a town's child come to preach in his home parish, by that face lean and austere as if with much thought on God.

The preacher rose, tall, his black gown round him, his bands white at his throat. He called the people to prayer. The elder's head bent, and from his lips came a thankful sigh. Time was when he had doubted ever to have seen Robert in the pulpit. For years now, since ever indeed he had been seriously exercised in spiritual things, the young man had had strange ways with him. And from the time of his dedication to the ministry he had not abandoned them, but rather grown set. It was not enough he should offer himself to distribute the church's alms to the deserving poor, but he must needs seek out the undeserving, frequenting the mean streets, nay even the taverns and brothels of the town, preaching there as if to the elect in church. Men spoke of the thing. And, dutiful son as he was, he would not depart from his practice even at his father's exhortation, giving for justification the words of Scripture, "I came not to call ..."

John Ritchie, the session treasurer, stood by the elder and coughed, bringing him with a start out of his dream. "I am ready!" the elder said. He gave but one more greedy look, then softly snecked the door behind him, and followed the other through the porch and down the five steps beneath and so along the churchyard path that led to the gate.

They knew their work. Each Sabbath day before the time of divine service it was the duty of each elder to visit his own proper district lest any should neglectfully absent himself from the means of grace. The elder had been very faithful to his flock that day: not a man or woman or child but was in the church where himself would so gladly be. But it was also the custom of the session, sworn enemies to sin and uncleanness and the breaking of the Lord's day, to send out two of their members abroad through the town during time of service itself, to rebuke anyone at all that they found extravaging the streets in idle companies, drinking in taverns, or employed in other than necessary works and ways. This day it was his lot and the lot of Ritchie thus to forsake divine service and go abroad. The elder sighed to himself: that it should have been this of all Sabbaths! But Robert was to preach the next Sabbath too; then he should sit at peace and see him with his eyes.

They passed into the Church Street. It was quiet and deserted as beseemed. Only as their feet rang on the causeway was there a hasty movement or two at the closeheads, the flutter of a plaid or of a skirt. The elder's first thought was one of sorrowful wonder: that any should be so blinded of the Evil One as to seek foolish pleasures, while in the church was pleasure incomparable! Then indignation burned within his soul. He tightened his lips and in his eyes the light of battle shone.

They turned into the Meal Vennel, and stood in consternation at what they saw. Some idle soldiers of the garrison walking with women in their arms and their plaids round them, two by two together, daffing and jesting. — The elder returned flushed to his companion's side. "I will delate them all before the session. Two are scandalous persons that have compeared before. They will be wiser than to forsake again the means of grace."

They turned next down the close towards the Dantzig Tavern and the elder knew no abatement of his ire. Two months before a member of session had been called "interfering dog" by the riotous company he had come upon. But the elder would be called devil and all and never heed it. He was into the place and over it, upstairs and downstairs, closet and parlour and kitchen. — He returned at length to Ritchie waiting outside for him. "The provost's cousin," he said, "Alas for it! Drinking with sailors and the cards spread out before him in a row. I will certainly delate him before the session, and Alexander Grant the innkeeper forbye for purveying drink to them, thereby inciting them to absent themselves from the house of God."

John Ritchie looked a little wryly at him. "You are very zealous this day," observed he. "I am, I doubt, but the smoking flax beside you."

On they went down the Bridge Street. And on the near bank of the river, half hidden beneath the first arch of the bridge, they came upon two men at work, Thomas Rait the fisherman and his brother, spreading out their nets to dry in the sun. The elder found great ease of utterance in dealing with them. But, leaving John Ritchie to finish the exhortation, himself crossed the bridge, for on the farther side he had espied a woman in the act of filling a pail with water.

She climbed the bank and set off along the River Street. The mud was thick, the elder might follow her noiselessly. She never in any case turned her head, but went on her way slowly, her shoulder drawn down by the weight. Through street after street the elder followed her, until she came to a group of old abandoned houses. She stopped by one and disappeared from his view.

The elder stood for a moment at the door to draw his breath. It was a mean lodging, too mean for a woman of good repute. Long grasses nodded in the rotting thatch, a pool of foul water lay around the threshold stone, and from within through a broken door came a dank earthy smell. The elder rapped on the door and pushed it open. As he appeared in the doorway the woman screamed.

It was a moment or two before the elder saw anything. Gradually as his eyes grew used to the dimness he saw the stool beside the dead hearth and some sort of bed against the wall. The woman stood directly facing him. She stared at him, her eyes large. In her arms, wrapped in some coarse stuff, she held an infant whose hand was spread upon the neck of her tattered gown.

"You are a mendicant?" the elder asked.

She answered him not a word, but stood staring at him.

"Without authority?" he sternly pursued, "You have come into the town without knowledge of magistracy or session?"

Still she said nothing, only moved her hands further over the child and turned a little away.

"Woman," the elder said, "What is your name?"

A step sounded. John Ritchie was approaching the door. "This is a way you have led me! I looked not, Master Sutherland, to see you so conversant with the stews of the town. Doubtless you have had one able to instruct you."

The elder bit his lip, but addressed himself only to the woman. "What is your name?"

She looked from one to the other of them as they stood barring the doorway. "Your name?" the elder questioned, "Tell us your name."

At last she said, whispering, "Elspet Henderson."

The elder frowned, "I wonder now, where have I heard the name? There was a woman came to my door, my servingwoman Janet did drive her away."

But Ritchie cried roundly, "Elspet Henderson! A harlot, lately banished town and parish. You have entered unlawfully into the town again?"

She said, "I had nowhere to go. No-one would take me in." She answered Ritchie but her eyes were fixed on the other.

"That babe you carry," Ritchie asked, "Is it a fathered babe?"

At that she bowed her head and began to weep.

But John Ritchie persisted, "Is it a fathered babe?" And the other, not to be outdone, repeated, "Is it a fathered babe?"

She said at last in a low pleading tone, "He can be fathered."

"Speak then: who is his father?" the elder asked. "It will go hard with you if you are not able to prove any of the town to be his father."

There was no answer, only her breath hissed.

"Who?" the elder went on, "Who? If you do not answer us, you will have to answer before the session."

Then suddenly the woman answered him. Flinging an outstretched hand in his face, she cried out laughing and screaming at once, "Your son! Your godly son that preaches in the church. Your own son!"

The elder's head reeled. He clutched the post of the door. As figures in a dream he saw the women, he saw Ritchie — Ritchie on whose visage horror strove with incredulous joy.

"Elspet!" the elder said helplessly, "Elspet Henderson! God lay not this sin to your charge."

The elder knocked with the tips of his fingers. "Robert!" said he.

There was no answer. He half hoped there should be none. If it were possible to avoid this thing! But now it was Thursday, he had held in the matter two days already. Robert had remarked once on his preoccupied air.

He knocked again, louder, and then again with desperation. The deep voice said, "Come in."

And slowly the elder entered his son's study. Upon the table lay a Greek Testament and his eyes dwelt with passion on the holy hardness of the lettering. And on the table also one slender slip of paper with Robert's small writing upon it. "Your notes," the elder said, and took the paper up. The slip was torn off one of his own used invoice sheets. "Is this all the notes you speak from?" he asked in wonder. "Is all else extempore?" His heart warmed within him. There would be no preacher in the land like Robert.

He looked covertly at him, standing with face pale, studentish, remote yet from prayer — for there was the broad red mark across his forehead where it had lain upon his hand for how long no man knew.

"Robert, sit down," the elder said. He himself walked to the window. Outside the sunlight lay upon the town. He could see over the roofs to where the river ran shining. The children played round their mothers trampling their clothes out by the water's edge.

The elder turned suddenly from the window. "Robert," cried he, "Women are troublous things. Through woman sin entered the world and I doubt through woman sin continues in it." The silence shamed him. "I knew one," said he, "far above rubies: your mother. Still and on, the generalty of women are liars and harlots born."

He looked over at the silent standing figure, and reproached himself anew. "I should not speak of such, and yourself preparing for next Lord's day." Then he suffered a stound of horror. Next Lord's day! And he had not yet opened the matter at all.

"Come and listen to me, Robert," he said, and went to a chair and sat down. "I cannot thole," he cried peevishly, "I cannot thole to have you standing there! Sit down, man, sit down."

"There is something amiss?"

"No, Robert, no," he said. "I was at the kirk session two days ago."

"On Tuesday."

"On Tuesday. We were detained late. Did you not remark on it?"

"It slipped me."

"We were late," the elder repeated with emphasis, "We were very late." How should he ever bring this matter to a head? — "What will your text be?" he asked, to put off time, reaching over for the slip on the table. "'I came not to call the righteous' — Robert! There is none righteous, no not one. — I was at the kirk session on Tuesday. We heard the pleas of those delated by John Ritchie and myself for misconduct last Lord's day. There was no great ado about them, the most paid their fines. There was but one — one Elspet Henderson, known too well already to the town, an orphan lass brought up by the master she served with, that ran from his employ and turned to evil ways upon the streets. Banished she was eight months syne from town and parish; and she is now entered by stealth into the town again, she and a month-old babe. She proponed she had no place to bide and the winter approaching. Setting aside the matter of her banishment, the session straitly interrogated her upon the father of her babe. Three hours were we at it, three full hours; and never a word else would she say but that ..."

He rose and walked angrily up and down the creaking floor. "The woman is mad, confused with much misery. There being certification out against her that no-one lodge or have aught to do with her, she has fallen into a destitute condition and is withal demented. How else could she so impudently persist in the thing? For being questioned and urged to make an open and ingenuous confession she would by no means give out any other to be father to her babe — but one as far above suspect as the sun in heaven.

"The session would have dealt with her as one obstinate, not confessing, and bound her over to the civil magistracy to be scourged at the town cross and banished town and parish, which will in any case be the way of it. Master Wilson himself, and the provost, and Stewart of Alvaig — and most part of the session would have closed the matter there and then. Only John Ritchie said ... Plague on the man! There was a cattle market at Chanonry that day, but see would he go to it!"

"John Ritchie said?"

The elder cried, "He envies me. He is thriven in trade, and a bailie, and church treasurer forbye. Yet hath he no son like mine. Maybe I have been proud. Maybe I have taken too much upon myself, righteous overmuch. But I was vexed they should not come and hear you preach."

"What did John Ritchie say?"

"John Ritchie said, since she did not actually keep silence but rather held to the one to be father to her babe, it were necessary for that one to compear at the church door next Lord's day as the custom is, there to purge himself by oath. For if not, said he, the man would go under shadow of blame all his days. And that is truth, Robert."

"What man?"

The room was full of silence. Only the roar of wind in the great chimney, and without a small crying of gulls upon the river, coming in over the town from the sea.

"Robert," the elder said, "Robert my dear, she says you are the father of her babe!"

He spoke on hurriedly, unable to look at his son's face. "The session will dismiss the charge at a word from you. And I would never have broken the matter to you, only ... only you were in the town last winter, Robert, it is known. Aye and resorted unto by the poor, and, even as you yourself admitted to me, by such persons as this. — It is your own fault!" he cried in a fury of pain, "I told you no good would come of it. It kept you from your studies then and now see what a bees' byke you have drawn upon yourself! Take not this text from which to preach, but take another that speaketh of touching pitch and of being defiled. — John Ritchie, whatever his motive be, spoke truth. An ill opinion of you would grow and infect your good repute in the town, even as one rotten apple on the shelf will infect all. And you new licensed, ready to be ordained — and to preach next Sabbath! I am glad your mother lies within her grave.

"Robert, I gave them my word you would compear. It is that that I have come to tell you. But it is for yourself to say. O what a strait we are in! Can you endure to be made a public gazingstock? Yet if you do not compear ..." He walked up and down again, stealing glances at Robert where he stood looking out of the window: the light was too strong for the glass to reflect his face. — "If you do not compear, they will say ..."

"Why, do not vex yourself," the calm voice replied, and the young man turned away from the window. "I will compear. Thus it behoveth me to fulfil all righteousness."

There was no need for the church officer to ring the church bell that day. The elder looked about him at all the folk. Upon the dyke around the churchyard sat the lewd ungodly, the soldiers from the garrison, their sweethearts with them, and ragged wild men from the Highland parts. Better for the session to be looking to their scandalous deportment than to stand here so staid and grave! Between the session at the church door and that company on the dyke the good citizens were crowded thick over the graves. "What went ye out for to see?" the elder said bitterly to himself. "O generation of vipers!"

Up the flagged path from the gate the officers came; between them came Elspet Henderson, her child in her arms. The soldiery and their women laughed amongst themselves and spoke from behind their hands; nevertheless they cast fearful glances privily at the constables that came behind, ready to take over the delinquent at the session's bidding against her correction on the following day. The good folk drew in their skirts as the woman passed them. The elder for his part noted with satisfaction her affrighted mien. She would have wandered blindly past the church door had not an officer plucked her by the arm. She stood below the church door looking this way and that over all the people. The child burrowed for her breast with a hungry cry.

Then from the church door came the son of the elder, and stood for a moment at the head of the steps, looking down over the throng. He had his black gown on as if ready for preaching; his bands fluttered white over his throat. He stood for another moment or two as if gathering stomach, then descended the five steps, and at a word from Angus Munro, the church officer, came and stood by the woman's side. He laid his hand, as was required, upon the child's head. There was some murmur from the midst of the people, and one bold laugh for defiance' sake from the dyke.

John Ritchie came and stood beside the elder. "A woeful sight this for a father's heart!"

"A woeful sight for town and session both," retorted the elder, "And one the latter might have spared themselves if they had a mind." He would doubtless have said more, but at that instant the words of the oath of purgation fell on the air. Angus Munro, husky and shrill with a sense of importance, read out the words in phrases, and in his deep voice the son of the elder repeated them after him.

"I, Robert Sutherland, now under process before the session ... for the sin of adultery alleged to be committed by me ... slander being repute as one guilty of that sin ... I, for ending the same process and giving satisfaction to all good people ..."

"He will preach yet!" the elder said to himself, "He did well to compear. None shall from henceforth open his lips against him."

"'... do declare before God and the congregation ... that I am innocent and free from the said sin.'"

"Do declare before God and the congregation that I ..."

Beneath his fingers the son of the elder could feel the beating pulse of the infant's head. He glanced down at the child and the mother.

"'... that I am innocent and free from the said sin.'" Munro repeated the words in an obliging whisper.

Under his fingers the quick hot pulse was beating. The child stirred, half asleep, half waking in his mother's arms. She herself stood crouched, her hands locked together to keep her hold on the burden growing heavier and heavier. The officers eyed her, the constables shifted on their feet as if ready ...

"Robert!" the elder said to himself in a fright, "O Robert, what ails you?"

"'... that I am innocent and free from the said sin.'" Once more the shrill voice rang out and the other forbore to follow. A low murmur broke again from the midst of the throng. The elder held his breath lest he should cry aloud. Ritchie had turned his head and was looking at him.

The son of the elder looked dumbly round about at the people. There was no sound now throughout the whole churchyard. Almost one would have said they were as quiet as those so quiet underneath their feet.

"'... that I am innocent and free from the said sin.'" Munro's voice sounded loud out like a menace.

The son of the elder looked again at the woman, for with a sudden movement she turned her face up to him. She cried, "Sir, it was one of the garrison men. I was very hungry. I gave myself to him for a shilling and a boll of meal. And three days after it he went to Flanders. Forgive me, O forgive me, for naming you! I was sore afraid and knew not where else to turn. For the child will die if tomorrow ..."

So deep the silence was the people heard.

The son of the elder finished hastily, "'... that I am innocent and free from the said sin.'" He signed to the people to remain silent. "This woman has confessed her sin," he said, "giving glory to God. Therefore, albeit I am not after the flesh the father of her babe, yet am I after a spiritual manner his father, and the session here is his father, being servants of Him who is a father to the fatherless." He turned and scanned the session with thoughtful eyes. "Master John Ritchie!" said he. "You are the treasurer. The privilege will be yours to make provision for mother and child. Let proper lodgement be found them, I pray you, with all necessary goods and gear. It is God's bounty," he added, with a warm smile upon him. "You will not stint."

He was away and up the steps and into the church. The elder stood bemused, till he was roused by the crowding of people past him. Without his bidding, the lewd and the ungodly went into the church that day.

The son of the elder . . . stood looking down over the throng

A Field of Peas

IT WAS THE year after the last of his children had married and left him that William Macdonald, known as William Oig, determined he would grow a field of peas. He and his wife both had a weakness for pease brose, a taste remaining from their humble youth; yet whilst the young folk had been at home they had not been able freely to indulge their predilection, pease brose seeming a little below that station of life to which William's success as a shoemaker had raised the family.

He heard from one of his customers of a little plot of land in the Millburn valley south of the town, on a gentle slope facing south to catch the sun; it was going cheap, and he dearly loved a bargain. So he bought it.

He had his two apprentices dig the ground and sow it with peas. — Fresh air and exercise is good for young folk, and it was in his time they were doing it, so he steadfastly refused their bold request for extra pay. Great was his pride and joy when, taking a stroll one late April evening with his wife, he noticed his rows coming up; and as the light lengthened he formed the habit of going there every evening to watch his plants grow. They put out tendrils, and the apprentices were called upon to work one or two evenings after hours setting brushwood supports. They grumbled, as boys will; but it was pointed out to them that this was a more beneficial exercise for them than playing football or camack. There came a day when purple flowers appeared. By the third week in July William gathered a handful of peas. He ate one or two, the rest he took home for his wife to put in their broth. He looked forward keenly to the time when he should get the whole crop plucked, dried and ground. He and his lady could have pease brose to their heart's content.

But at this point things began to go wrong. One evening when William went to see his field he found that some other hand had been plucking peas for some other broth. One hand, or more? The latter seemed likely from the extent of the depredation; and the thieves had gone heedlessly about it, many of the plants being trampled down. He went home vexed to his wife. Is it not very hard when a man may not enjoy the fruits of his toil?

It was not enough for him to confide in her, he must needs confide in his customers, and in his two apprentices who listened with respectful sympathy.

"It maun be the birds, master," said round-cheeked Rob, who had been but a few months at the leather trade.

"Put up a bogle," sallow Tom advised.

To whom William somewhat testily replied, "Birds do not trample pea plants down. It is folk passing by on the road."

"We'll take a stroll there, if you please, master, now the shop is quiet?" Rob was only too eager on a summer's day to lay down awl and thread. "If we see a body so much as put a hand to them ..."

"Get you on with your work," William commanded him. "I might myself, however, take a turn that way when I am fitting Kingsmills with his shoes."

But though he went that day, and he and his wife on several others, they never saw anyone at the peas. Yet the spoiling went on. It became clear the thieves were coming by night.

One day William had risen early and gone to Millburn before work and found so much of his crop gone that he was absolutely enraged. As who would not be? In his shop he swore an oath for all to hear: "I will be even with them yet! I'll lie in wait for them. And I'll have my gun."

His wife was aghast to see him set out on this grim errand instead of coming doucely to his bed. It did seem a drastic penalty to exact, but in fairness it must be said that William, though called Oig or Young, was getting on in years and would be no match for stout young fellows if it came to fisticuffs.

He had to wait till it was nearer twelve than eleven before the northern twilight dimmed to night. Then he set off with his muzzle-loader gun and enough small shot to pepper a score of thieves. He took up his position between two rows at the top of his field. And there he waited, lying on the ground with his plaid wrapped round him for fear of the dew.

... There is nothing like solitude for drawing hidden thoughts up into a man's mind. When he heard melancholy hooting, though he knew it to be owls on their nocturnal occasions, he felt the sound had a note of foreboding in it that made the hair rise on his spine. What if robbers came who were desperate men, escaped from prison or galley, who would stop at nothing? What would his wife say when his body was discovered ...? — He should have taken one of his lads with him.

Perhaps he dozed off. At any rate, something roused him. He became aware of distant figures moving silently along the road by the burn. Two, three, four ... how many he could not judge, for they passed in and out of the trees, now in starlight, now in shadow. He rose to his feet to watch them. Travellers maybe, on their way south? But he recalled he had once heard that travellers were known to shun this valley after nightfall, preferring to spend the night in town and set out on their journey the next day. What was it he had heard given as the reason? He could not call it to mind. But he felt he had been perhaps a little foolhardy to choose this particular place for his agricultural endeavour. The very fact that he had had such a good bargain of it struck him now as a little sinister.

What, they were leaving the road and coming into his field! They had emerged from the trees, and were plainly to be seen: three, four, or five ... they were moving too close together for their number to be exactly ascertained. The thieves? The thieves! Taking what another man had laboured for! Anger overcame fear. Come on then, the lot of you! Here's something that will make you jump. Just you come on, my mannies, and you'll get a surprise. He dropped on to his knees, arranged powder and shot in the muzzle of his gun, rammed it all in, and took aim for the middle of the group. When to let fly at them, at what moment? Should he not let them start their plucking of his peas, then take his sweet revenge?

He was puzzled that they were coming so directly towards where he knelt and not straying here and there for peascods. His finger was about to draw when he noticed another strange thing: they were not dressed in men's attire, their garments showed them to be women. What would bring women here? He held the gun at the ready, but forebore to fire.

The figures looked unearthly tall, their height increased by high pointed hats. — Strange! They looked like pictures of ... Then suddenly he recalled why this valley was shunned at night. Down there, where the burn spread out into a wide pool, he could see a ruined house outlined against the sky, an uncanny fragment of a house, gable and half a wall. It had been the house of the notorious witch Creibh Mhor who, a generation ago, had been burnt at the stake for casting a spell upon Cuthbert of Castlehill.

It was horrifying how the company came on so confidently, without any attempt at concealment. Indeed they had come for other thing than peas! They were talking and laughing among themselves, if one could call their high shrill babbling speech, or their eldritch howls laughter. He tried to deny it to himself, but by his beating heart and sweating palms he knew they were women who were as they should not be. Fool that he was to come here alone at night. And for peas. For peas! He would have given all the peas in broad Scotland to be safe in his bed.

O may they not notice him, may they not find where he crouched behind his leafy palisade! He laid his face down on his arms lest its pallor gave him away. But they had come expressly to find him, incensed no doubt at his intrusion into their unholy domain, and they knew where he was. He heard their feet coming near and nearer. He made out the words they said.

O, was it possible? He imagined he heard his own name. "... William Macdonald, the shoemaker in Baron Taylor's Lane ..." They were talking about him. — His trembling hands were trying to steady the gun. — Lead would not dare upon hides fortified by the Evil One. A silver bullet ... but where could he ...? He laid down his gun and searched feverishly in all his pockets.

And as if they read his mind the crones screeched out: "Och, have no fear. The old skinflint willna have a sixpence on him."

"Eppie lass?"

"Gang in ahint him, Meg!"

"Take him at the back, Ishpel. Where are you?"

"Here, sister, here."

They were all round him, encircling him, cutting off his escape. When he tried to slip between them they would close in together, waving their arms with catcalls of glee, so close to him he would hear them snuffling, reaching out hands ...

"What will we do with him?"

"Give him the pox."

"Make all his teeth fall out."

"Off to the Plantations with him."

"Catch hold of him! Catch ... I've got him!"

A skinny hand had caught him by the plaid. There was a roaring in his ears, blackness before his eyes. He heard a loud shriek, and felt the shattering impact of the ground.

When his eyes opened, he did not know where he was. He got wonderingly to his feet. He saw the little valley, green, with the rising sun glinting on the blue Firth beyond. He saw his field of peas. And into his consciousness rushed the horrifying happening. He must have fainted and fallen and lain unconscious. Fainted? Maybe he had died? His persecutors must have judged him dead to have left him alone. Was he still alive? Intact? In his right mind? He held up a hand and counted the fingers. Five. Yes, he was lucid enough to count them. Though he was cold and stiff and trembled violently, all in all he was himself still.

The relief turned his terror into fury. How dared they? How dared they practise their wicked art here, so near the town, in the very valley which had been purged by fire? How dared they trespass on to his field, threaten the rightful owner with being transported? He picked up his gun and staggered a few steps. A new insult rose in his mind. How dare they call him skinflint, him a decent thriving man?

He set off for the town as fast as he could go. He knew it was very early by the stillness of the streets. But he would go and report this scandal. No good going to bailies either, it must be straight to the Provost.

Bridge Street was deserted; no movement anywhere but the river's. The Provost's house was altogether shut up. William lost no time in beating upon the door; when this brought no answer he took off his shoe and thumped with that. A window opened upstairs and a tousled head came out. A hoarse voice bade him hold his noise, the door would be opened.

The Provost appeared, hugging a bedgown round him, sleep still in his eyes. "What's all here?" Then, recognising William, "Guidsakes, Shoemaker, you're making an early call!" His eyes went over his visitor, dishevelled clothes, wan face and staring eyes, and over the gun. "My Go', what's up, man? What's up? Is it a riot?"

"Worse, far worse."

"What said you? Worse nor a riot?"

William stepped to his ear; he could hardly bring the words out: "Provost, sir ... a case of ... witchcraft."

"Now, now!" the Provost shook his head and smiled. "Now, now, you're not serious. This is the age of Reason, sir. Such beliefs belong to one that's past."

"Man, I'm telling you." William here began his story. He had not gone far in it before the Provost stepped back from him and was clearly in a mind to put a closed door between them.

"This is hardly my business," he said. "If it's as you say, you would have done better to lay the matter before the ministers of the town."

"I thought it was your business. I have come straight here."

The Provost had his hand on the door, ready to close it, but William besought him, "Sir, I am not well. I must sit down and recover my senses a little."

Grudgingly, then, the Provost let him in, and with hand upraised for silence in the house, led him into an inner room. There a dram partly restored him.

"I am thankful," William said, wiping his brow, "that I sit here in the presence of the Provost in my right senses, a denizen of this town, instead of being ..." His voice faltered.

But he had spoken better than he knew. The Provost puffed out his chest and said, "Have no fear, sir, have no fear. I will hear your story, however strange it be."

He sat and heard it to a finish, by which time he was pouring out a dram for himself.

"Now, Shoemaker, is there anybody whom you suspect? Have you no inkling of who those women might be? Have you never had dealings with any whom you might suspect of forbidden powers?"

"I have no dealings but with respectable women."

"Tush, man, I know. But have you never among acquaintances, or customers say, become aware of a woman whose appearance ...? Any of whom perhaps inadvertently you might have cheated ... wronged, I mean?"

As William looked offended, he went on hastily, "Well, then, was there nothing about the women you saw that could suggest their identity? Five, you said, or six or seven? Of what stature were they? How were they clad?"

"I have told you. They were ..."

"Yes, yes, yes. We need not go into that again." The Provost's hand had strayed towards the decanter. "The problem is how to set about looking in a town of this size. We might perhaps begin by making inquiries of several households as to whether a female person was absent during the night."

William rejected this. "They are said," he whispered, "to be able to leave a semblance of their bodies behind."

The Provost drew his gown in to him. "Hem. Well then, my dear sir, but you must give me something more to take hold of. Made they no reference to any person?"

"Yes," William answered dolefully, "They referred to me. But wait! They called to one another by name. Meg, I remember. And Ishpel. And ... was it Eppie?"

"Common enough names. Still, they will afford me some clue at least when I put in train my inquiries. I am glad," he said, rising, "you came straight to me, and I hope I shall always be able to deal with the cases of our loyal townsfolk as swiftly and decisively ..."

Here William cut him short: "Indeed, Provost, I shall be able to say so only when you have found the culprits and brought them to justice. To condign and exemplary justice. I trust that you and the Town Council will give yourselves no rest ..."

"Leave the matter to me. But remember, it is a delicate one. We must proceed with the utmost caution. As far as discretion will allow, I will leave no stone unturned."

With that lukewarm assurance William had to be content. He went home to report his adventure to his anxious wife. He left his business to the apprentices till the afternoon.

If you want something done you are best to do it yourself. William said nothing to anybody, though he craved sympathy, but he kept his ears and eyes open. More than one of his neighbours and customers remarked upon his altered manner, his sharp penetrating scrutiny, his strange riddling questions to them. Whatever business he was at, his secret concern with every woman he met was, "Is she one of THEM?" A question which was followed by one even more disquieting, "Is she likely to vent her ill-will on me again?" He felt tolerably safe, so long as he did not go near the Millburn valley. Still, if not for his safety's sake, then for his satisfaction, he must find out who the guilty women were. His wife could not but hint at the reason to those neighbours who spoke to her of her husband's ailing look. She did not pass on to him their gloomy prognostication that he would from now on go farther into decline.

A week went by and he was still in the dark. Then, as he was returning one day from a visit to Drakies, whither he had gone to fit Mr Munro with new riding boots, as he was approaching his shop in Baron Taylor's Lane, he heard loud boisterous laughter and shrill voices raised. It was so reminiscent of that night in Millburn that his heart missed a beat. But it is one thing to meet witches when you are alone and in the middle of the night in a haunted valley, quite another to meet them by day in the concourse of a busy street. His heart grew still. He stood where he was and listened.

"Get ahint him, Meg!"

"That's you, Eppie lass."

"Where are you, sister? What will we do with him?"

"Give him the pox. — Take out his teeth, he will need his brose then! Off with him to the Plantations, the old skinflint."

In the intervals of the jeering came whimpers and appeals for mercy in a quavering voice. His own! — Furious he strode round the gable and discovered his own two apprentices sitting on the low wall, together with three or four others from the street. They were rolling in their mirth, heedless of anything but their game. It gave the outraged William the chance to get in some shrewd blows on their heads.

The other boys eluded him and were off down the street, pelting one another with peascods. But his own two had no escape; he had them cornered in the workshop where luckily no customer was. He could only stutter. He did not know with what to tax them first, wasting their present time, damaging his field, threatening a citizen of the town or trifling with the powers of darkness.

Sallow Tom tried to make some insolent reply. Rob could not speak, his mouth being filled with peas.

"You shall hear more of this!" William left them, to work if they would, to play if they had a mind.

The Provost was entertaining one or two of the notables of the town. He was little pleased to hear that a petitioner required his ear downstairs, less so when he saw who it was.

"It's yourself again, then, Shoemaker? What news, man?"

"I've found the guilty men."

"Men, did you say?"

William would have gone on at length only the Provost stopped him.

"Enough, enough, my dear sir. You have convinced me. Well, well, well, well, to think your own boys should play such a trick on you!" He had begun to smile, and seemed on the point of laughing outright, when he noticed the unsmiling countenance. "What! Are not you relieved? Now that you know who the culprits are your mind is at rest."

"At rest!" bawled William. "I will not be at rest till I get my revenge."

The Provost glanced up the stairs lest any head should appear over the banisters. "I doubt, sir, for your own sake we should leave the matter alone. This is an age of Reason, we should be laughed at if it were thought we had intended to bring a charge of witchcraft against anyone. As to your peas, I will see you are compensated for them. Good day to you."

And he left the unsatisfied William at his door.

He was, however, as good as his word, so far as it went. But William Oig and his wife had grown somewhat averse to pease brose, and long before midwinter they were glad to bid their apprentices cease from bringing them peasemeal at the rate laid down by the Court of half a peck every second week.

... all round him ... cutting off his escape ...

A Game of Camack

A BEAUTIFUL DAY. O truly splendid weather! The river ran sparkling to the firth which lay all blue below its surrounding hills in their green and russet, with Ben Wyvis looming above, white with an early fall of snow. The air was crisp and clear, a fresh wind blowing from out of the Great Glen. A beautiful day for any time of the year, but for November a wonder. It was such a pity, young Tom Matheson said to himself, it had to come on the Sabbath! His fingers within the broad pockets of his best mulberry-coloured coat closed as though they held a caman.

His eyes met eyes which held a like thought to his own. Here came Colin Macrae and his young brother Fergus, and Jack Forbes loosening the tight cravat round his throat. The boys loitered together without speaking, at any rate in words.

"Make haste, what's keeping you?" The stentorian voice of Tom's father was modulated as all sounds had to be in honour of the Day. Tom sighed and moved forwards after his parents; the others after theirs. There was a crowding of folk from west of the river upon the bridge, delayed by the paying of the toll. The boys stopped again and felt in their pockets. A bodle is a small thing, one sixth of a penny, made to be lost in the lining of a coat. They stood slapping their sides. But Tom's hands were on that imaginary caman again, and young Fergus had taken a round wooden ball out of his pocket instead of a coin. He stood meditatively throwing it from one hand to the other.

Geordie Crom the tollman was taking an awful time, giving out change maybe to those too elevated to carry a mere bodle on them, or else daffing and passing the time of day, Sabbath or no. The boys had perforce to stand and wait.

Across the river was the High Kirk, awesome, the bell from its tower echoing along the valley telling all the folk it was service time. Many had already heeded the summons: Bank Street was dark with them, hastening, hastening, whole families hastening together like a human river flowing alongside the real. Lucky they were, those east-of-the-river people, who could go to the Kirk on the Sabbath scot-free!

The bridge was of stone, all seven arches of it, built thirty or forty years before, still the pride of the town. The only thing against it was it had cost a great deal of money and, though Lovat and the Chief of Macleod had handsomely contributed, the town had been left with a large residue to pay. How else could they discharge this debt but by asking a trifling sum from those using the bridge? Tom Matheson's father was a bailie and he accepted the necessity. But there were some in the town, as there will be in any town, who muttered that they thought the Council had no call to be imposing any toll: they were against it as a matter of principle. Some, indeed, went so far as never to make use of the bridge at all. They would rather pay two bodles a week to a woman to wade across carrying them upon her back. A matter of principle, they said, though in view of the lowness of the remuneration they offered it might be as much a matter of interest.

But on this beautiful and inviting day all four boys and another half dozen or so silting up behind them felt the reasonableness of this refusal to pay the bridge toll. Fergus was still casting his wooden ball from hand to hand. Across the river they could recognise the red head of Hector Morrison, captain of the east-side camack team whom they were to meet for their annual camack match on New Year's Day. Yes, that was Hector, and more than one of his team must be with him, wending their way doucely along the river, to sit for two and a half mortal hours completely still. Ah, what an advantage it would be to have an extra practice …

If you have no bodle to pay, or if from principle you will not, how else can you cross a broad and rapid stream? You cannot wade across, lest you stain your Sabbath breeches. It is not every Highlander who wears a kilt. You would think shame to be carried by a woman; in any case the women are all in the Kirk today. You cannot get a boat and row across because there is no fishing and the boats are all lying bottom upwards at Friars' Shot.

So then what are you to do?

The bell was giving out its last summons, its peal falling slow and irregular with warning: come now or be late! As they stood listening moodily to it, Fergus by accident let his ball fall from his hand. It rolled seductively over the grass of the bleaching green, and their eyes followed it.

The bleaching green was empty; no women there to spread out their shirts and gowns in the sun. It stretched along the river's course, shaped to its gentle curve. There were two posts partnered nearby for those who preferred to hang clothes in the breeze, and farther down another two ... or was it one post and a tree? At any rate, the whole lay-out of land suggested to them ...

Colin and Fergus who lived nearby ran home and came back with their camans. They brought two that were spare for Tom and for another young fellow who lived two miles away. It was a matter of moments only before they were taking good cracks at the ball, passing it from one to another along the ground. And what harm? They had the whole place to themselves. Only the very old and the very young remained in the nearby houses. The only one who could testify against them was Geordie Crom and everybody knew that, once he had mulcted the godly, he would fall asleep, his beard resting on his breast, his bag of bodles between his feet. So there was nothing in it. They had ample time for a little practice: when they saw the Kirk door open and the worshippers issue forth they would hide by the bridge and join in the throng returning westward; with luck none would be any the wiser. Tom aimed for the open space between the posts; Colin fiercely defended. The cracks of their camans on the ball toned in with the crisp exciting air.

By the time the rest had been home and were back with their camans they were spoiling for a game. Tom threw up his caman and the rounded end fell nearest to Colin, so he got first pick. He chose Jack right off. But Tom got Fergus. Six on each side, no great number; but better than nothing. They tossed a bodle and Colin got choice of wind. He said his side would play downstream.

Tom threw up the ball and the contest began. At first it hung

equal, with strike and parry on the ground. But then young Fergus
got the ball up into the air and ran through his attackers, and fleet as
a hare sped down the bleaching-green, twisting his caman deftly to
contain the ball within its crook. The rest came bounding after him,
to hinder or support. But he was alone, ahead of them all, when Jack
Forbes, standing "cul" between the clothes post and the tree, rushed
out at him. Fergus faltered, but with a cunning feint he sidestepped
his opponent and shot the ball triumphantly through. It was only a
half hail. Still!

Without delay the winning team turned round and moved in the
opposite direction. Here they met difficulty. Even Fergus, hero of the
hour, had to admit within himself that their success had been largely
due to their having the wind at their backs. Now with the wind in
their faces they found the going slow. From side to side of the green
they went. They had no eyes for what their feet were doing in the
way of tearing up turfs of grass. One would not give much for any
sheet or towel a goodwife might let fall the following day!

Once the ball was shot to the brink of the river. It was brought
back with the question, "High or low?" "High" it was, so it was
thrown up into the air. And this time it was Colin who almost
equalled his brother's feat by carrying the ball to within a foot or two
of the enemy goal.

But Tom's team was the stronger, for even with the wind in their
faces they drove through the posts and up as far as the bridge,
converting their half into a hail. Colin's men would not let it end
there, however. This time they claimed advantage of wind, and took
the ball if not to the other goal then very near it. In the heat of the
battle they sustained various injuries, a black eye here, a cut lip
there, a staved thumb, a bruised ankle. But all went unnoticed.
Their only pause was when once again the ball was shot off the field
right into the water.

They leant, panting, on their camans, watching the player who
went to retrieve it ...

And then they saw a sight which instantly cooled them down.
Women, their skirts tucked up above their knees, their boots in their
hands, were wading back across the river to the west side. And a long
dark cavalcade of folk was moving upstream, their pale faces turned

all to the one side. Heavens! Divine service was over; the kirk had scaled. They had been playing in full view of everyone! The boys stood petrified. They might drop their camans, but the din of their shouts and playing hung still in the sunny air.

They went dejectedly up to the bridge. It was no longer a case of their trying to hide from their parents. Their parents hid from them ...

The minister himself came, still in gown and bands, his session at his back like retainers of a chief. They practically constituted a kirk session meeting there on the green. At any rate, it could be said that a preliminary examination of the crime was made.

To wit: himself who may, for all his absorption in higher things, have remarked the slight diminution of his usual congregation, opened with the question, "What for have you been absent from the means of grace?"

They severally deponed they found themselves unable to cross by the bridge, there being a toll to pay.

Master Macintosh, session clerk, inquired, "Was it the case they found themselves without a bodle?"

Whereupon himself breaking in, a little impatiently, inquired, "Was there no other way open to them to cross? Had they not heard — they had heard with their ears but not with their hearts seemingly — how in a sermon preached two months since he had made mention of the godly Strathnaver men who crossed a river when it was in full spate ..."

One or two of the accused here broke in, deponing there were no wading women available, it being the Sabbath.

Others, as being ashamed of the implication, added that had there been a boat they might have rowed over, but the fishing cobles were laid up upon the Shot.

Himself, impatiently, again resumed. — The Strathnaver men, of whom he had made mention, had waded across the river when it was running in full spate; not one had let such a small consideration as comfort or safety or the preservation of his garments deflect him from his duty. Had it not occurred to any of them to wade?

They variously, in humble tone and with relevant action, pointed out their Sabbath clothes, some showing some diffidence, however, observing that their fine raiment, if not wetted by Ness water, was stained by the sweat of their game.

"You will hereby observe, sir," said Fergus, "it had at least been our original intention to sit under you today."

Himself, as somewhat mollified, made to those nearest some observation upon the sins and faults of youth. The session clerk, however, obdurate still, demanded afresh, "Had they, including in their number the son of a bailie, been so destitute as not to possess a single bodle?"

Upon Tom Matheson's remaining silent, answered on his behalf Colin Macrae: it was the principle of the thing that withheld them from paying. Was it right that a tollman should be employed by a town on the Lord's Day?

Upon this, there was amazed silence on the part of the minister and session. The young men were commanded to compear for judgement upon the Tuesday following at seven in the evening.

Our party had sober faces when they did compear. Stern fathers had prophesied a variety of dooms, among which featured the branx, the cutty stool and the stocks. Fond mammas had wept.

Himself cleared his throat and commenced. Their trespass, he told them, he would treat of under TWO HEADS.

FIRST: the playing of camack on the Sabbath.

Whereas, himself said, it had been, and in certain parts of the country still was, the custom to indulge in camack upon the Sabbath — he himself had heard of a parish, not so far away, where it was the practice for the young men to drive their ball all the way to the kirk and all the way back again when service was over ...

Young Fergus at this point with bright eyes inquired, "But how, sir, did they score a hail?" Himself, with more tolerance than might have been expected, replied that the side that was stronger chose to play towards the kirk. — But that was mere supposition on his part, he had not permitted himself to watch such a Sabbath game.

Fergus here asking, "But how would they know which was stronger before it was decided by play?" The session clerk reminded those present the culprits were here not to ask but to answer questions.

Whereupon himself, clearing his throat again, intimated that, not to leave the matter in doubt, they would proceed to deal with the FIRST HEAD.

For the transgression of playing a game of camack on the Sabbath the young men must consider themselves rebuked.

The young men were vastly relieved, a rebuke being, after all, a thing of air, no pain or discomfort in it, and, as soon as one is released from one's rebukers, no shame.

There remained the SECOND HEAD.

To wit: the absenting of themselves from the means of grace.

They had made it their defence that it went against their consciences to pay toll on the Sabbath, thereby causing a fellow man to work on the Day of Rest. Their tenderness of conscience, he said, was a credit to them and to the parents who had so godly brought them up. They had, indeed, awakened the Kirk herself to the fact that she had been committing a sin. "Ex ore infantium," he said, with a glance round to see if any understood. There was therefore no penalty, not even rebuke, on this head. Here and now he would make known to them a piece of news, which would greatly please them. — The good man himself, indeed, looked highly pleased. He positively beamed on them, and answering smiles came upon the boys' faces. — The session had met with the Town Council last night. The Council had listened favourably to the crave of their petition: which was that on Sabbaths the levying of a toll upon the bridge should cease. Utterly cease. From now on, without respect of clan, name or other appellation, all lieges should pass over on the Sabbath entirely free. The town could find means of making up the deficit, and have as reward the knowledge that it was honouring the Lord's Day.

"Yes," the good man said, "from now on you will pass freely over and with clear consciences attend."

His face beamed; the faces of most of the session beamed with his. Was it not strange that the faces of the boys fell?

A Mortal Man

GEORGE BISSET SHOUTED farewell to his wife; she was busy in the field behind their house, turning the flax to get the dew of the coming night. And he gently extricated himself from the embraces of his two youngest children. "Papa cannot take you out with him," he explained to James, "He is going to the Town Council meeting." The boy's mouth went down: what can a child of four years old understand of the importance of such a thing? The baby Bisset had simply to set upon the floor, putting a sugar bool into the mouth opened to cry.

He gave himself a hasty dicht where the children's fingers had left marks upon his best dark coat, and set his blue bonnet straight upon his head. Elspet was at the door by now, gathering back the bairns. She watched him go with a face of loving pride. He was not very tall, not very handsome, and certainly not very modishly dressed. — Ah, if only he did have a fashionable coat and Southron shoes! But the needs of a family must be met before the parents get anything. — Still, his face showed him good and amiable — and he was off on business of the town.

Watched by her loving eyes, he went up the vennel towards Church Street. His progress made little stir. Most passed him without any other greeting than a mere tilt of the head. Others vexed him by casual orders or complaints relative to business and out of keeping with his present status as town councillor. "Have you that length of fine linen ready for my wife yet, Master Bisset? She is eager to have it made up into handkerchiefs." "George Bisset, it is not the case that I am owing you four shillings on my bill. I settled it in full last time."

Some gave no greeting at all but looked sourly at him. Bisset was not surprised to see, therefore, crossing the head of the vennel, the Deacon of Weavers, on his way, like himself, to Council but, unlike himself, in splendid buckled shoes. That Deacon was his evil genius, wherever he went putting folk against the proposal to set up a linen manufactory in the town, against the linen industry itself, and particularly against Bisset, a master handloom weaver and now the prime mover for the setting up of the manufactory. Humble by nature, Bisset was uneasy himself at his rise in status and had little resistance against the other's often expressed opinion that he was a common working man and nothing more.

Now, seeing his adversary only a little before him, he drew his head down between his shoulders, for on the whole he was a lover of peace. But he went on his way and turned into Church Street.

He tried to keep to the crown of the causeway to avoid the puddles and horse droppings that clogged the sides, and as he went he wondered within himself whether some day the cleansing of the streets might not be effected by some public authority and not, as now, farmed out to whomsoever thought his kitchen garden would be the better for manure. Left to private enterprise the work was done slackly, according to the needs of the gardens and not according to the comfort of the lieges on the streets. He had on one or two occasions ventured to express his view in Council, but he had been laughed at for his pains. — Elspet never fully understood why it was her husband came back from Council quieter than when he went, as if humiliated.

Our linen worker, however, returned that night from Council enlivened by the piece of news he had to tell. His voice woke all the children and they rose on their elbows to peer from behind the curtain of the boxbed. The Lord President of the Court of Session was recently returned on vacation to his native town. Yes, the Lord President was of this town: he had been born here and sent to the Grammar School. And he delighted in coming home. Now what had he done but sent an invitation to the entire Town Council that he would be happy to wait upon them at dinner at four o'clock on Wednesday of the following week! The Town Clerk, who had had the agreeable task of passing on this invitation, described it as "a patriotic desire upon His Lordship's part to elevate the functionaries of his native town in the scale of civilisation."

You may be sure the invitation became the talk of the town. There were those ill-natured enough to declare that the Lord President was too free with his invitations, but they were those not included in this particular one. To those who were, it became a preoccupation, from the Lord Provost and bailies down to our humble friend. Many in those intervening days were plainly observed to be practising behaviour. What affability all of a sudden was seen in the low bow of this bailie, what a graceful carriage that councillor was seen to display! Even the Deacon of Weavers was so ready with his smiles that he smiled once upon Bisset by mistake. Their women were chiefly concerned with the matter of dress. And here poor Elspet was at a loss to know what to do. The Provost and bailies had their mantles and chains, those not so magnificent at least had coats of reasonable newness with waistcoats to go with them. What could her husband do? She knew he would have no finery other than a new white linen shirt.

But he himself could think of nothing else than that he was shortly to be in the company of the Lord President, who had been a hero with him for many years. He listened to everything he could pick up about him: he knew of his patient working with the Highland chiefs doubtful of their duty to the king and their duty to the Stuart cause; he thrilled to the story of his bold championing of the city of Edinburgh when she was like to be deprived of gate and guard after the lynching of Captain Porteous. How clear-sighted he was now in scenting out abuses in the practice of Law and in putting them right, as when he brought in the rule that no cause should lie before the Court for more than five years. And how merciful — had he not said it were better to suffer twenty guilty men to escape than condemn one who was innocent? Ah, what a wonderful thing it is in a man, not only to see what is right but to have the power to put it into effect!

The front doorway stood between the pillars at the height of four steps, the windows set in beautiful symmetry on either side. A tranquil and gracious house, its beauty struck Bisset even as he stepped modestly round it to the back door. It was only when he heard a sound of voices and turned that he saw two or three of his fellow councillors coming together in at the gate and making their way to the front door, and realised there lay his way too on this day of days. He gave a glance at his brogues, and before stepping further he took his bonnet off and rubbed them with it. He felt a sharp dig in his ribs and straightened up to perceive that his fellow guests were all bowing.

There was a lady to greet them, in a silk gown, with winking jewels on her neck and in her hair. And then his head whirled, for there stood the President. Tall, six foot and more, of a slender build and of noble carriage, he took the eye; and now he had a smiling genial face, a face of holiday. The Town Clerk at his side announced the names of those arriving. He said Bisset's name in a rapid heedless tone which could not have made it audible to the President's ear. Since one of the bailies had to be announced immediately after, it was perhaps not to be blamed on him. A quick handshake and smile, and Bisset found himself passed on with the rest. If only he might come near enough to hear his host speak before the evening was out!

They were ushered into an anteroom and given a dram. The linen worker felt he had need of one; his forehead was wet with sweat. Summoned to dinner, they went in procession into a large room with looking-glasses lining the walls. Reflected in them he could see the portly Provost and the Dean of Guild next to their host. There was ... yes, it was the Deacon of Weavers following hard on their heels. And among the rest, appearing from behind stout old Bailie Schevize, a drab insignificant fellow he realised must be himself.

In the middle of the room was a long table covered with a white cloth — his own handiwork: he recognised it with a stound of delight. On the table was an army of silver and glass that sparkled to make the eyes blink. Bisset sank into a seat and felt bemused: among all the forks and spoons which was he to use? Fingers would have sufficed him at home, and his good sgian dubh.

There was a call for silence and the President said grace. Then it was, "Take up, gentlemen!" Followed a squeaking of chairs as the company settled itself more comfortably to comply. There were slippery oysters, and broths which he enjoyed, salmon — common enough in the river town — roast beef and a ragout. There was white wine and red. If only he might pouch a little of this abundance to take home! Once indeed he did reach forward his hand under cover of taking up his glass and removed a comfit from a silver dish; but even though the action went unobserved, he felt it below the dignity of such a table, and dropped it back in.

His chief concern was to hear what was being said by the Lord President. He was too far away to hear clearly, he was aware only that the great man was telling anecdotes of the Bench: one could judge from the faces of his listeners when the tale was grave and when droll. Bisset leant forward, straining to hear, though on one side he was being deaved by the prosing of Bailie Schevize on his perennial subject of the fishing rights on the Ness.

And then occurred an untoward incident which interrupted even the Lord President. The Deacon of Weavers, upon smelling the various delicious odours, was suddenly minded to sample a dish of tea. He had heard of this new modish beverage and felt sure that one of these odours must belong to it. It would at any rate, he thought, make an impression upon his fellow councillors were he to show a predilection for it. He summoned the butler with a vulgar tilt of the head and in a loud voice bade him instantly bring him some TEA. The butler did not feel he could deal with so untimely a request by himself and he approached the hostess, explaining it and asking what he was to do.

"Can he not wait till we are in the drawingroom, John?"

"He says he wants it now, your ladyship."

"This is strange. But you had better ask for some to be made."

"Now, ma'am? In the middle of the serving of the dinner?"

The President's lady sighed, but a guest's wish was law. "Serve it from the sideboard."

In due time therefore the Deacon was called from his roast beef and invited to serve himself to tea from the sideboard, where the butler had set out the silver teapot, the sugar and cream, and the precious china cups and saucers. From his cup the Deacon took his first experimental sip. — And was utterly disgusted. With his disgust there entered into his mind an aggrieved sense that he had been summoned away from the table as being thought unfit to sit at it. His hand trembling with passion, he reached over to place the cup and saucer on the sideboard again. How much was design and how much accident who could say? But cup and saucer went flying, with another cup or two for company, to shatter with a resounding tinkle upon the wooden floor.

The sound interrupted the buzz of conversation; all heads turned that way. On the hostess's face there appeared a look of pain, though only for a moment. As for the guests, the Town Clerk's face went crimson, the Provost sat like a statue with his forkful of beef suspended midway to his mouth. The Deacon stood transfixed, unable to move from the scene of his disgrace. The President himself came to the rescue. With a good-natured laugh he cried out, "Well, well, Deacon! It cannot now be helped. I must make the shuttle pay for it some day. — Take up the pieces," he bade the spellbound servants, who then ran with faces of horror to pick up the fragments of my lady's cherished Meissen.

There was a squeak of chairs: the guests were rising to their feet for the ladies were leaving the table. With the same opening of the door as let them go, there went the hapless Deacon of Weavers. The linen worker would not have been human had he not felt some satisfaction in seeing his adversary so put down.

There was at any rate a more genial atmosphere after his departure. The Lord President motioned his guests to come nearer to him. Bisset would not of himself have dared do any such thing, but old Bailie Schevize rose and shuffled forward, drawing him after him. "Come, come, sir! Let us not be backward in going forward." Suddenly to his amazement he heard himself spoken of by name. The President was conversing with the Provost, who then raised his voice to call, "Master Bisset? Where is the linen weaver, Geordie Bisset?" Guests anxious to assist thrust him forward, until he found himself seated two or three places from the head of the table.

— "Is that not so, Master Bisset? It was your proposal, I think, that the streets of the town be cleansed at public expense?"

There was a titter of amusement from more than one of the councillors, but the Lord President looked round at them with a frowning seriousness that hushed them. "I am greatly taken, sir, with your idea. I wish you success in carrying it through. Should it be so carried, I look to see the example followed in other burghs."

Bisset's ears burned. He could say nothing in reply. He had the feeling he was floating, his humble head among the stars.

Then, after further chat, the President rose to his feet; clearing his throat he began by saying there was little enough the capital city had to offer their own beloved town. "I believe there is but one thing," he said with a boyish grin, "but one material thing which they possess in abundance and we do not here. Well, let us not be too vain to follow a good example." With an air of mystery he clapped his hands, whereupon the door behind him opened and in walked half a dozen men bearing in their hands boxes of a peculiar three-cornered shape. The President laughed at the curiosity visible on every face. "Gentlemen! I have taken the liberty of bringing North with me a selection of HATS, in the hope that some of you, if they desire and can find one to fit, will accept one as a gift. No, it is nothing, gentlemen! A mere bagatelle. I beg you will forgive the liberty I have taken and do me the honour of trying on one or two."

Whereupon the hatters opened the boxes and drew out marvels of their art that made the councillors gasp. Such glossy nap, such elegance of shape, such subtle variations the one from the other. — Even the Provost, who had a cocked hat of his own, held up his hands in wonder.

There followed a strenuous quarter of an hour, during which the hatters went from one to another, to achieve for each councillor a perfect fit, striving to gratify one man's desire without frustrating another's. The President strolled among them, indeed it required his diplomacy to allay the pangs of a guest whose hat had been in an instant whisked from off his head.

Lucky were they who had come riding to the Lord President's. A cocked hat, when few have ever been seen in the town, requires a horse if not a carriage to do it justice. But there were more than one, among them our linen worker, who had come on foot. They would without doubt be subjected to rude quizzing.

Their host sensed their difficulty, and arranged with one and another of the carriage owners to provide rides home. To Bisset's incredulous joy he was offered a place in the President's own. To sit in the seat of so noble a being was an honour to cherish for the rest of his days. I dare say that was the only thought in his head during the time it took to reach the point where his vennel turned off Church Street.

But once there, when he had requested the coachman to stop and had alighted, he became conscious of what was upon his head. The coach turned and went home; he was left alone to run the gauntlet of his neighbours. Indeed they were there ready for him, the sound of the horses' hoofs clop-clopping on the cobbles having alerted them. He was used to their whispering disparaging remarks to one another behind their hands, while calling out ironically to himself.

But now as he walked towards them, his hat on his head, there was silence. No jesting, no ironies: only a silence which from their expression was plainly one of awe. On he came. And still they gazed at him. Old Mistress Ross as he passed her made a bob. Simon Mackintosh the tanner touched his forelock. Before long six or seven men together were doffing their blue bonnets.

Elspet ran out and stood gasping, sobbing with surprise and delight. She loosed her apron from her waist as if it were unseemly to receive her transfigured lord with it on. Their daughter came with the baby in her arms: when he saw his father the child, like Trojan Hector's, wept affrighted at his awful head. Bisset, like Hector, snatched off the too terrifying headgear. He clasped his trembling wife with his free arm and, near to tears himself, he cried out, "O good folk, why do you gaze so upon me? I am a mortal man the same as yoursels."

One Day in the Life of The Swordsman

IT WAS NOT so much the cold, Alexander Grant said to himself with whatever part of him was awake and lucid. He had often before spent a night in the open, rolled in his plaid like this, when out rounding in his father's sheep on the Braes above the Glen. At thought of Glen Urquhart, lying so green and quiet, he was lulled again to sleep.

But he woke when someone on the ground beside him sobbed in his dreaming, and began to go over things again. It was not so much the cold that took the heart out of them as the hunger. — Now he was fully awake.

The hunger, and the fatigue. He himself felt this less than the young chap beside him, young Macmillan from the Braes, who had scarcely made the return journey from Nairn before he dropped to the ground. But he felt the hunger; and now, between sleep and waking, he dreamed of meals, meals eaten warm by the fire, shared meals and Margaret sitting opposite him at table with the light of the fire flickering in her bright hair.

Peace. His mouth was drawn into a smile. How far away was peace now, from him and from Margaret. She was no longer in Glen Urquhart. She lay at Aldourie, at her father's farm. He had had to leave her in the very hour of her great need. — And here where the tired dispirited men lay by Culloden House there was no peace: the smell of faction among their leaders in the nostrils of the men was felt as fear.

Who was right? Lord George with his declaration they should stand on the south of the Nairn River, if at this time they should stand at all, or the beloved, the Prince, who said *here* and *now*?

Whatever was done must be done with the disapproval of one or the other. Just as when first he felt the desire to lend his sword skill in the service of the exiled King he had had to harden his heart against the opposition of his chief. A sad business when a man's own heart is divided, torn between this duty and that. But the sons of his lesser chief, his kin, his cousins — they were in the righteous disobedience with himself.

All would be well. — If only it could be soon over! This end watch of the night, so brief to the exhausted sleepers, was long to him now fully awake. If only it could be soon over, and the ordeal at Aldourie over. How this same hour must seem long to Margaret: when would he be free to win back to her?

So it was almost with joy that he heard the flurry of feet and hoarse shouting, agitated calls and commands in two languages. He got to his feet and intercepted one of the men who were running here and there. The English army were on the march, they had got within three miles already. No time now to choose another battle ground; it was here and now of pure necessity.

Like a manifold giant the camp woke; bugles rang out, pipes snored and sang. Men came running together from the whole area round Culloden Park, tightening their kilts round them. Grant put over his shoulder the plaid he had used as a blanket at night and fastened his sword belt. He felt happier with his sword on.

The bleak April morning seemed reluctant to come; mist and rain filled the chilly air, with sometimes a stinging shower of snow or sleet. It was blowing from the east, in their faces, behind the backs of their more fortunate foe.

Grant counted his followers and placed them with his cousins'. They were to stand with the Frasers, Chisholms and Stewarts of Appin on the right wing. Leaders appeared, mounted on horses, seeming higher because of the drifting mist: Lord George, one of the Irishmen, Lochiel. Then there was a great doffing of bonnets. A young man had come, sitting upright on his horse, the light sufficient for them to see his fair head. A murmur of love ran like a flame among the cold men.

The Prince spoke: in the English tongue with a strange accent, but with a gaiety that was plain to understand. "Here they are coming, my lads; we'll soon be with them. They don't forget Gladsmuir or Killiecrankie, and you have the same arms and swords." He took up the sword of the soldier nearest him. What he said more Grant did not hear but a wave of enthusiasm now ran almost bodily, a fire, through the clansmen.

They would have begun their attack forthwith, only the order was passed among them to await the exchange of artillery. For an hour they endured the fire which opened lanes through their ranks like clearings in the wood. Death came suddenly to some. The rest, tormented, stood where they were and waited.

At last word was given to charge. — Or was it given? Had word been given at all? The wind blew stinging sleet in their faces, they had to lower their heads with bonnets pulled over their brows against it. Even so there was a wild delight in the running over the heathery ground. Grant had his musket ready for the first attack, but scarcely had he fired than he shifted and took out his sword. Here he was in his element. His skill was so great that he was nicknamed The Swordsman. He was conscious only of the space in front of him, filled with red-coated soldiers whose eyes widened upon the charging clansmen, shouting and whirling their swords above their heads. They were through the redcoat lines. They charged on, when suddenly the fire of the guns engulfed them. It came from behind the enemy foot. The whole world was blotted out in stifling smoke.

The Swordsman's feet stumbled over an obstacle. Glancing down he saw the fallen bodies, some inert, some writhing. Again the fire came and again, its smoke engulfing them. War shouts were mingled with shrieks and groans. The Swordsman grunted as once and again he clove his way through the redcoat ranks.

So dark it was, with mist and smoke, he could scarcely see the gleam of their bayonets, but he saw one go into a fallen Atholl man and come out red.

They were through the first line. Raked by cannonade they ran on.

Someone shrieked at his side. A Highlander, a Macdonald perhaps, had gone down upon one knee under a musket shot and now waited the finishing-off thrust of the bayonet. The trooper's right arm rose in the air. In the same moment The Swordsman's rose above it. He brought his sword down, sheering off the arm before the bayonet found the Keppoch man.

He whirled the sword round his head to protect himself now. For he was in amongst the enemy's second line. The redcoats were thrusting the clansmen back, back. Or rather, the deadly cannon thrust them back. The redcoats ran all between and around them. He attacked wherever he found one against him, which was all the time. His sword was kept busy! The sooner it was over, the sooner the event would emerge. Like a birth.

Smoke cleared; the enemy foot were fewer around them. Then the dire reason was revealed. They had withdrawn on purpose to give room to the cavalry, who now charged, high out of reach from the ground and by that the more dangerous. Their horses' plunging hooves trampled the fallen into the wet ground.

Retreating, the Highlanders were raked again and again by the gunfire. Stumbling back, over one another they fell, and rose if they could to stumble back still.

A voice cried, "Alastair!" The Swordsman glanced down, and saw his own brother with a face of clay, the blood from a wound in the shoulder bubbled out from between the fingers of the hand he clasped it with. Kneeling beside him was his shepherd boy and a retainer of their cousins'; in their distraught faces was the knowledge he tried vainly to reject from his own mind.

"For God's sake," Alexander panted, "Take him out of this. Get him to Cradlehall to my father's sister. Let him die there at least."

As he stood upright again he saw a horseman above him, his arm uplifted. He was too late in defending himself. The blow fell on his head.

His state of confusion, darkness, pain, was like a woman's in difficult labour, hovering between life and death ...

He cried out in remonstrance as hands jerked him, jerked his dazed and throbbing head. But some instinct bade him allow himself to be pulled along. He was out of the thick of the fighting, out of the centre of carnage, and saw with astonishment the wide wet moor and the lines of low hills. — The moor was littered with bodies.

He found himself running, together with a band of men, some his own. "To the town, down to the town," some cried, "Hide in its houses." Others cried, "No! They'll trap us." They argued it as they ran with wheezing breaths.

They came to a little cottage by the roadside. Young Macmillan who was wounded and losing blood and very thirsty stopped and knocked on the door. A woman came, with staring eyes. "Deoch, deoch, a'bheinn!" he gasped, and she held her pitcher of water to his mouth. As some woman will hold water to Margaret's —

The thudding of hooves brought them to their senses. They crouched by the gable, and the troopers went by following the road but fanning out over the adjacent fields, netting any prey they saw on the move. Two farmer's boys who stood gaping at the redcoats were hewn down ...

The others plucked Grant by the arm and he awoke from out of his trance of horror. "Are we to hide in the town? They're ahead of us, we'll be surrounded." They looked to him, The Swordsman. He had become their leader. It was true, none knew the lie of the land as he did. He led them south by Culcabock, then south of the Crown hill, by Culduthel to the height of Drummond. Though in their weariness they balked at the steep descent to the river bed, he drove them down, to the wooded valley where, bright and clean, the river ran swiftly among its islands.

The men wanted to rest there, to get their breath, and, hidden as they were from the Castle on its height, it seemed safe enough. But from the town, borne on that same easterly wind which had harassed them on the Moor, they heard random shouts and cries, the crackle of musketry, the sound of horses.

As they waited, panting, the sound of horse hooves sharpened. Along the track skirting the course of the river dragoons were coming. Even this spot would not be spared.

Grant called his men upstream to a ford he knew. But they said they were too weary to attempt to cross. They would rather die where they stood. He fell into such a passion, however, that they followed him into the cold swift waters. The chill added to the pain of wounds, the swiftness of the currents added the last finishing touch to their exhaustion. Once Macmillan went down, and it took all the fury of The Swordsman to persuade him to struggle on again.

Shouts came from behind them. Their splashings had been seen by dragoons following up the course of the river. They had drawn them as a racing hare draws the dogs after it. Balls whistled past them, missing them by a hairsbreadth. When these stopped, Grant turned to see, and found the dragoons must have spent their stock of powder and shot on their way through the hapless town, for they were firing no longer. But three of them set their horses into the river, standing high on their stirrups, waving their swords round their heads.

On to the western bank — there to lose oneself among bushes, slip into cover like a secret animal, to find a way up the Ness to ... Himself needing no other spur, he urged on his despairing comrades. But they were still in the river when one of them screamed out that the foremost of the dragoons was on them. Macmillan, hampered by his wound, could not go quick enough. He was floundering in the water, the horsemen standing high over him making ready for the kill.

Grant did not know he had turned back, but he found himself back in the stream. His sword whirled up and cleft the horse's head clean through. It shrieked once only, then its huge body plunged sideways. The rider went down in its splashings; he had not touched the river when The Swordsman struck a second time. The current flowed red a moment or two.

Appalled by the fate of their comrade, the rest of the dragoons stayed in the water at the river's brink, as if debating what next to do. Grant had his band in shelter of the trees and bushes that surrounded the parkland of Bught. From there he led them through the trees, sometimes nearer the river sometimes further away. At one point, beyond the Sandy Braes, he made them cross it again, threatening them savagely with the flat of his sword when they showed reluctance to obey. He could not tell them, for it was no more than a dim instinct in his exhausted mind, that the object of his journey was Aldourie. He must get there. And with him he must carry these weaker companions of his.

But as he won nearer his goal he wondered whether it were hope or fear that drew him. What could be born safe on so inauspicious a day? There must be black disaster everywhere, and universal defeat. All the more reason for him to get quick to Margaret.

The going was hard, through country thickly wooded. But the April night had scarcely fallen when he got them on the path that led, an easy clearing, through the woods to the grassy haugh beside the narrow neck of Loch Ness. All of them were in straits, famished, utterly exhausted, hardly conscious. If they could but make the houses on it, where they would find shelter, a meal served by kindly hands, help in dressing wounds! He left them at the first house.

He himself went to the farm, Margaret's girlhood home, his steps slowed less by weariness now than by apprehension. The image of the battlefield littered thick with dead and dying, his brother's mortal wound, the deaths he had that day himself inflicted ... He could scarcely bear to enter the house, seek her room, where the inmost core of all death might be —

The elder trees in the garden he could not see, nor the small yellow flowers that starred the ground, but he smelt the fresh smell of damp foliage. Night and rain had silenced the birds, but there was a familiar comfortable sound of munching from the byre. He had his hand on the latch of the door, but still could not bring himself to go in.

Silence in the hall — or was there a murmur of soft voices, subdued laughter? Then unmistakably he heard the small high short cry of the newly born. Swiftly then he went to the bedroom. It seemed tiny after the wide countryside. Yet all life was in it. For there lay Margaret, alive, safe, flat under the coverlet. The neighbour skilly woman was stooped over a cradle which stood before the fire.

He would not have dared go in, after such violence, such defeat; but she became aware of him standing in the doorway, she put out her two arms for him, and he went to her and kissed her. Her shining eyes directed his and he went to the cradle. "A boy," the skilly woman said. "A son for you. Born less than an hour since. She had a long labour."

"Charles," Margaret said in a voice still weak and high. "His name is Charles." Her face, still gleaming with her sweat, was radiant. "My father said it should be that name if it was a boy. And you will approve of it?" His silence struck her. She said with a momentary uneasiness, "I have not seen my father. Since last night he has not been about. And you yourself gone. — It was like a battle."

It gave him his chance to tell her. "A battle indeed, my dear! We made our stand beside Culloden House, but we are utterly ruined. Those that are not killed are scattered. The Prince is fled."

She did not seem to understand. Her eyes did not lose their blissful look; around her pale lips the smile still hovered.

He said roughly, "Margaret! Do you understand? We were defeated this afternoon. The Prince has had to flee. We are all undone."

Then she woke from her trance and cried in alarm, "Your head! O Alastair, there's blood all over it." She got up on an elbow, then sat right up and encircled his head with her arms. The skilly woman cried out in reproof but she did not heed her. "There's been a battle?"

"We are straight come from it, I and a few men with me. The redcoats are out everywhere in pursuit."

Now at the open door there were footsteps, she gasped in fear, but Grant knew the urgent voices. "Swordsman! Come! Take us to the hills."

"I'll have to help my lads away. I'll have to hide them. I know places above the Glen where they'll never be found."

Women brought broth and bread, but he had not time to take them. He stood stroking Margaret's damp hair. The men cried again from the door. "Swordsman! Hasten! We must not be caught here."

He leant down and kissed Margaret, "I'll be off then." Yet his energetic words were mocked by the lethargy of his limbs. He could not stir. What might become of her until her father returned, if ever he did return? What might happen to her, left here unprotected except for a neighbour woman? What if these innocent folk were involved in the penalty hanging over those who had fought on the battlefield? He saw before him again the dragoons cutting down the two country lads.

"Swordsman! Alastair!" again from the door.

He was the Swordsman, the Protector. — Yet whom should he protect if not this woman, weak and spent and unable to rise yet? The mother of his newborn son? He must send the rest away — let them fend for themselves — and himself stay.

O but better for her if when the redcoats came they did not find her in company with a man so plainly fresh from battle! For her sake he must go, for her sake.

Yet his limbs would not move.

It was she who drove him away. She put her two arms against him and with weak strength pushed him from her. Even when he made a move to peer again into the cradle she cried to him to be gone.

So he went, and found the shelter of the hills above his Glen, while across the Loch along Wade's road to Fort Augustus the redcoat dragoons were constantly to be seen. He lived among the hills, carrying in his mind what he had had no time to take up in his arms, the little son who had won his victory of birth on the very day when the Prince whose name he bore had suffered such sore defeat.

The Swordsman . . . clove his way through the redcoat ranks

The Jail Dancing

JAMESIE CUMMING LAY with his hands behind his head and from floor level watched his fellow prisoners. They were hauling up their bags at judicious intervals, drawing them through the window grating, and eagerly scrabbling inside to find what the result of their street fishing had been. For the most part they were woefully disappointed. The good folk of Inverness seemed to have grown weary of charity. One bannock of oatcake and a heel of hard sour cheese were all the takings for an hour by the steeple bell.

Himself he seemed no longer hungry. They said some got beyond it. Or was it that he was hungry for other things? When he heard it flowing in the stillness of the night, he was sometimes sick with longing to see the River, and the fields of the Bught beyond it, and the woods of Tor Vean. Now and again, for a treat, he would let his mind roam further, to the rising moors over which he might one day go, back to his mother's country of Speyside.

Not that he could any longer entertain himself with the plans for escape which had solaced his first hours. — The Badenoch outlaw had knotted his sheets: though he had dashed himself to pieces upon the cobbles below he had known the sweetness of breaking free. But in the Debtors' Prison where were sheets, or blankets either, or mattresses other than armfuls of straw? — Some had been known to change clothes, but he had too few left him for purposes of exchange.

Sometimes he thought that what he hungered for was only his fiddle. The men shut in with him pined for sweethearts and wives, groaning at night with passion unfulfilled. And he groaned with them, for the smooth curves of his fiddle between his left hand and his chin, and the feel of the bow submissive to his right hand. His fiddle!

Jamesie moved his head restlessly upon his arms. He did not grieve to see his coat go, nor his plaid brooch, nor his buckled shoes. It was no more than just to take those to pay part of his debt. But to take his fiddle ...

If only he could win that back! He vowed he would never get himself into such a pickle again. It came of being soft, so his uncle had told him. He had scorned to take anything for the food and drink he gave to the wandering fiddlers who came by, asking nothing from them but a new tune to learn. He had run up a fine bill at Shoochgar the grocer's. Folk said it was a shame to put him in prison for this; some of the bailies even were on his side. But Shoochgar, a bailie himself, was on good terms with the sheriff ...

There came the sound of locks yielding, the creaking of the outer door of the jail, then heavy steps on the stair. Visitors! The prisoners hurriedly hauled in their empty bags and rushed for the door yowling like dogs frantic for food. The door of the Debtors' Chamber slowly opened. Tackety Tamson the senior jailer stood there, blinking at them morosely and swinging his big keys. Sure enough, he was ushering in visitors. Jamesie got to his feet for they were for him, his uncle and cousin; and with them was Bailie Shoochgar himself: of course, it was said he haunted the Debtors' Chamber, hoping to win back his dues.

"Ech, but it is a sore sicht for a kinsman's eyes, this!" the bailie was saying, "to see his own sister's son languishing in the jile." He cast a significant glance round at the fouled and rotting straw and at the stocks and the pillory housed here for convenience. "If only you could see your way, my good sir, to a monthly payment, it wouldna take but till the next spring."

Momentarily Jamesie's heart leaped with hope. Here, after all, was the surest way to get free, his debt to be paid for him.

But he knew how it would be. His uncle stopped the other. "Na, na, Bailie, the thing's not possible, sir. I would but spoil my own business. Besides, every herring maun hang by his ain tail. He is of age: he is all the man he will ever be."

There was the jingle of Tackety's keys and Bailie Shoochgar's heavy steps again upon the stair.

"Aye, aye, Jamesie!" his uncle said. "This is indeed a fine place to see a member o' the family. It's a mercy your poor mother my sister lies in her grave. It isna every uncle would go the length of visiting in such a place. Peech, what a noisone stinking place it is!" Not anxious to linger he came to the point. "We canna exactly let you starve, your aunt's got too much feeling. We've brought you this." He pulled his pale son forward and from him took a package which he thrust into Jamesie's hands. "See now and turn your back on the rest while you eat. Mind what happened last time, they fell on it, tearing it from my hands."

Jamesie knew before looking what the contents of the package would be: boiled salmon, cold greasy stuff; they would have bought it from Peggy Raff's flyblown shoppie opposite; it was in season and cheap, a penny a pound. Even the prisoners would think twice before stealing it.

"Many thanks then," Jamesie said wearily.

"Well, if that's all, we'll be going. See and be good. See and not be learning worse at any rate."

The young cousin was sickened by the jail smell. His father took him by the elbow and led him away, rapping smartly on the door until Tackety opened it. Jamesie gave the salmon to the Ross-shire men who had been cleared from their homes to make room for sheep.

He must have dozed off, for the evening sunlight had shifted round on the houses opposite the grilled window, when there was a sound of quick light footsteps on the stair, making a counter rhythm to the slow heavy steps of Tackety, and a clamour on the landing outside. Then came the creaking of key in lock. The door swung open. Into the Chamber plunged three young men; and Jamesie got up again, for he saw that the foremost was Jock Rose, the senior bailie's madcap son whom he had met at parties in the taverns of the town. Behind Jock he saw Fergus Macdonald the surgeon's son, and Peter Wishart.

Jock was arguing with the jailer. "Losh, what harm will it do?"

"It's against the rules, Master Rose, against the rules."

"There isna any rule against visiting the debtors. Did I not see a party leaving a while ago? Forbye, Mr Tamson, a man like yoursel' is able to use his discretion." Tackety Tamson gave a sniff, liking the respect. At last he went away, leaving Jock and his companions inside, though shaking his head, and giving the key an extra hard twist in the lock by way of improving the situation.

"It's glad I am, sir, you do not come as prisoner here."

The young man laughed, throwing back his head, a particularly handsome one. "No fear of that, Jamesie. I'll jink them all yet."

"What takes you then to such a place?"

Jock put his hand on his shoulder. "What do you think? Why, man, we've come to visit you."

The boy must have read his thought in his face, for he drew in a breath, then said gently, "Na. I doubt I havena brought the sillar for your freeing. I spent the whole of my cash on something else."

Jamesie felt a pricking behind his eyes: it was not only the sharpness of the disappointment but also the contrast he could not but observe between the gaunt men of the jail and the sleek young gentlemen of the town. Jock seemed again to read his thoughts. "Indeed, Jamesie, it's I am sorry to see yoursel' here. Braw fiddler that you are, it's a sinful shame. They willna do the like to you when your name is made. But cheer up, man! The world hasna come to an end. We've brought you a bite of food."

Fergus at this brought out from inside his cloak a basket, out of which he took large portions of roast meat that still bore the fragrance of the oven. There was enough to give most of the debtors a small share, some luckily having taken the edge off their appetites on the salmon. There was also a roasted fowl or two. Not from Peggy Raff's this, but from the tables of the Rose, Macdonald and Wishart establishments — and what their mammas said about the loss it were best not to enquire. To wash it down Peter Wishart pulled out from his pockets a couple of bottles of claret.

"Well now, Jamesie," Jock said, when he thought his friend's appetite was satisfied, "Look what's here." He shook back his cloak ... and suddenly the whole world changed: the squalid chamber might have been a palace. For under Jock's arm what did he see but his fiddle, his own.

Jock nodded his head as he put it into the owner's hands. "Aye well, that's where my money went — and maybe a wee bit of my father's. What for no? What better would he himsel' have spent it on?"

He glanced away from the ardent look of gratitude, being a

modest young fellow enough. "What, Jamesie, then? Are you in the mood to play? — Guid's sake!" then he cried, "Has the auld deevil harmed it? He had a notion to give it to his grandson, an imp of four year auld. It's Shoochgar the grocer I'm meaning; I bought it back from him."

"Na, na. O na!" Jamesie lifted his head and drew his bow questingly over the strings. He tightened one. "It isna harmed, it's fine." Then with a ring of authority in his voice he asked, "What will I give you?" He tightened another string, gave a few more experimental sweeps of the bow, and then went softly into a tune. One or two of the prisoners looked up from the bones they were sucking.

The fiddle was like a live thing. It laughed and wept. A small glowing came upon the prisoners' pallid faces. Some rose to their feet. As for the boys, they could not keep their feet still.

"Well," Jamesie said then, "What about a strathspey? Here's one I picked up from an auld blind fiddler in Grantown."

To the slow time of the strathspey the boys took sliding steps, giving a spring when the gallant music played the sudden snap. Upon the foul and littered floor they went about fairly dancing.

Jamesie turned into a reel. The boys took hands and danced round and round upon the middle of the floor. Faster the fiddle went, faster went they. One of the prisoners, who had been in the shortest time, came forward and joined them. Another followed him. Jock Rose kicked the straw out of their way; then, to get wider room, they all pushed the stocks and the pillory into a windowspace. They looked less formidable that way, indeed ludicrous: the boys flung their bonnets and cloaks over them.

They were so lost in the fun they did not hear the door open, but they saw Wullie Wotherspoon the prentice jailer standing with mouth agape. "Losh be here and mercy on us! Music in the jile!"

"Here, Wullie," Fergus said quickly, thrusing a shilling on him. "Gang down, man, and get us a jug of ale. That's you!" Wullie responded to his push rather than to his words, and went, though not before locking the door well behind him.

The boys looked round the prisoners. "Four of us — five. We need eight altogether." The music of the eightsome reel was so urgent they could not keep their feet still even while the circle of the dance was not complete. Most of the prisoners, though willing, were unable to dance, being too shoogly on their feet; but one took his place on the floor, and that made six.

And there was Wullie in the doorway again. As if lured by a spell he came goggling in and dumped the jug upon the floor. "My certies, dancing next!" Belle Tamson, Tackety's daughter, his sweetheart, was peeping behind him.

"Here's the two more," cried Jock. "And one of them a lady."

"O losh, is it me?" simpered Belle. Wullie stood as if transfixed, but she was already on the floor, waiting for him. Round they went, the eight, this way and that, then set in couples one to the other..

They had scarcely got their breath back at the end of the reel before Jamesie struck into a strathspey for the foursome that should follow.

So loud was the stamping and hallooing it brought up the two merchants whose premises were on the ground floor below the jail. Bailie Macintosh had an inkling there was something going on for it was to his wine shop Wullie had applied for the ale. And with him was Mr Spence, a chandler, a worthy sober man. Their shouts of horror brought upstairs their wives, with a daughter or two clinging to their mothers' skirts.

"Get back down, lassies, there'll be an injury," cried Bailie Macintosh.

But the ladies thought otherwise. "'Deed it's no riot this. It's a kind o' a dancing."

Mr Spence was aghast: "Dancing, and in the jile!"

"What for no?" cried Mrs Macintosh. She was a lively women, not much past middle years, and her toes had begun twitching. "That's a grand fiddler, whoever he may be. He has the look o' a prisoner on him, but hoch! it's only for debt. Do you ken his tune? It's 'Stewarton Lasses'."

"Aye well," her husband answered, "I must say it's a good tune. Did they no dance a reel to it at our wedding?"

"Faith and I could dance to it again."

Such a charming hint could not be ignored. The bailie took his wife by the waist and swung her into the middle of the floor, where they did the figure of eight and the chain as gracefully, almost, as on their wedding day.

"Do not you be looking at them, Elspet," the chandler said to his own wife, "for it's maist unbecoming."

To which she replied, "I ken it's unbecoming, but it's awful nice. Jean!" she bade her daughter, "Run down and tell Jennet to mind the baby. I will not be down for a wee whilie yet."

"And tell our boy to send up candles," cried Mrs Macintosh, who had all but slipped on the floor. "And tell him to bring me up my smelling salts, for the prison smell."

Her partner was wiping his brow. "And claret. It's drouthy work this. Bring's up three bottles, they needna be the best."

The candles made a good shine; at any rate Mr Macintosh could see to pour his claret. "Here's to the fiddler!" he gave the toast. Then he gave another, "Here's to us all here, whether bond or free."

Mr Spence scorned to call a toast but he drank his claret standing by the wall.

Then they fell to dancing again.

In the midst of this there was a cold draught from the door and a loud roaring from Tackety Tamson who strode into the chamber. He had to bang his keys upon the wall to get any attention at all. "Guid's sake and mercy on us! What's going on here? Wullie Wotherspoon, are you out of your senses? Jock Rose, you randy, this is your work! Oot o' this, the whole clamjamfry o' ye, oot o' this. Everybody that's no in here for debt, get oot at once."

"Hoch, what's the harm, sir?" Jock said softly to him. "We are just going in any case. There is a soopie o' claret still in the bottle. Will you do us the honour of taking a drop o' it?"

The jailer sniffed and considered. "Well, then, to please you."

To please them further he had another. And to add still to the pleasure, another again. Then he joined them in the next strathspey, leading in Mrs Spence. Who could do other? 'The Tailors of Elgin' was irresistible. No human foot but must start skipping and hopping. The jailers took the merchants' wives, the boys their daughters. Mr Macintosh even took Belle Tamson, while she giggled into her plaid. The prisoners danced with imaginary wives and sweethearts. Mr Spence in the end succumbed to 'Mally Paterson's Reel', dancing alone, his feet looking as if they had no connection with his sober face.

No sooner was one dance over than the company clamoured for another. Even if they were tired there were no chairs to sit down upon, and Jamesie played as one possessed. He gave them jigs to vary the reels and strathspeys. When the candles burned low they sent down for more.

More candles.

And more claret.

The noise could not be contained in the Debtors' Chamber. There was a prodigious kicking upon the inside of the Thieves' Chamber door. "If they're complaining o' the noise," Tackety instructed his prentice, "Tell them to thole it. They're not paying for their keep and maun take what comes."

Wullie on his return, however, reported, "They're only complaining they're no getting in to the dancing here."

Whereupon Tackety, outraged, went himself and kicked back on the door. "Keep quiet, you rascals, will you? Dance where you are."

The noise could not be contained within the jail walls. It pervaded High Street and Bridge Street. Folk passing stopped to listen. Many a casement window, for all the chill night air, was thrown open and heads stuck out. "Where's yon music coming from? My, but that is the grand fiddling!" More than one pair of lovers under cover of the dark stole in and up the jail stair, and, finding the door hospitably open, joined the merriment.

Bailie Shoochgar the grocer intercepted the Provost who was taking his nightly stroll about the town. "Come till you hear what's going on, Provost! I'll walk along Church Street with you, for it'll be a shock for you when you reach the jail. Forty-seven years have I lived in this burgh and nineteen of them have I been a bailie. But never have I heard such a carry-on in a decent jail. And the people crowding about on the causeway below, it's a fair scandal. It'll have to stop, Provost! There'll be no terror in the Law if this goes on."

"Aye, aye, it must stop, it's most unseemly," agreed the Provost, when the sound of music grew in the air. "What is't? Is it 'Major Lawrence's Fancy' or 'Mistress Aitken o' Dunbar's Reel'? Who in creation's playing? I didna think we had such a bonnie fiddler in the town. Ta-RA-ra-ra-Ra-ra-ra-Ra — Is't no bonnie? — Go you home, sir," he said as they turned into High Street. "Do not be affronting your ears with such a thing as this. I will send those idle folk away."

His presence did his work for him: so soon as they made out his form in the dim light the crowd who had been capering and dancing melted into darkness and left him alone. Whereupon the Provost took a few dancing steps all to himself, before going regretfully down Bridge Street to his house, which had the town's insignia upon twin lamp-posts at the door. And all the rest of the night till he went to bed he listened neither to the low voice of the River nor to the high voice of his wife, but only to tunes beating merrily in his head. And as he went to bed his thoughts dwelt upon the idea, how pleasant it would be if some day he got a tune called after himself. Till sleep overtook him he amused himself making up titles for it. 'The Provost's Fancy', 'Provost Robertson's Strathspey' or, maybe, 'Provost Robertson of Inverness'.

The watchman had cried one o'clock of the morning. Bailie Rose heard him as he went about the dark streets looking for Jock who was not in his bed. He did not know whether he wished to meet the town's officers or whether he wished to avoid them. He was certainly taken aback to run right into them as he turned into High Street. Under the jail they were dancing a figure of eight, with their lanterns swinging from their hands. One of them, flown with gaiety, called out to him, "Is it your son you're looking for, Bailie? Has it come to such a pass you've got to seek him in the jail?"

"Hold you tongue!" cried the indignant bailie, "I would not have come this way but that the noise o' you drew me. Whatna carry-on is this? Go about your business. No, dinna talk to me o' minding the jail. We have jailers to mind the jail, it is for you to mind the town."

He saw them off on their several ways, flashing their lanterns industriously into close and vennel, before hurrying himself along Church Street. He had tried the Dantzig Tavern and The Horns, but in vain. It must be in some private house that Jock was playing at the cartes, spending good money. He was as eager for his father's money these days as one time he had been for his mother's milk.

The dancers need no music now, they dance to music running in their fuddled heads. They cannot stop dancing.

The key is in the lock but the door stands open wide. Out on to the landing ... No shouting from the Thieves' Chamber, no hammering on the door. Listen and you will hear only the muttering of men in uneasy sleep.

The door that guards the stairhead is open too. So now down the stairs. Stone does not creak. But take care! What was that sound from the merchants' premises on the ground floor? Only the fretful crying of a child for its mother, and a word of peevish comforting from a maid waked from her sleep.

Ah but the outer door? It is closed. But not locked. What lies outside, though, in the street? The night officers may be passing at this moment; they are known to keep an eye on the jail. Peer out and see. Nobody. The street is vacant under its pall of night. Not a footfall, only the muted beat of the feet of those still upstairs dancing.

Down Bridge Street. Careful where the doorways jut out, a pail or a pile of rubbish ready to trip unwary feet. Past the Provost's house with its lamp-posts shedding a dying light upon the cobblestones. There is a little crack of window open: is that the ghost of a chuckle, a movement of a bed where a sleeper lies whose toes are dancing in a dream?

The Bridge ... There is a bodle to pay. But all is well. The watchman lies in his small shelter in deepest slumber.

Now to the fields and woods and friendly hills.

The jailers were not the first to come to their senses. The merchants, with a prudent consideration that tomorrow would soon be here, had taken their hot and weary wives and daughters downstairs to their beds. Jock Rose and his friends remembered they had to climb in at their bedroom windows before dawn. They went out and left silence at last behind them.

Only the debtors remained, asleep on the floor.

"Go', but this is an awful thing we have done, Wullie," observed Tackety to his prentice. "It was you led me into temptation, though I should have kenned better at my age. Howbesoever, it's no great matter if they're all here, the craturs." He held the remainder of a candle up to count heads.

All were there except one. Jamesie the fiddler had vanished with his music. They went round and round in growing agitation. But he was not anywhere.

"O lorry! What are we going to do at all?" quavered Wullie. "It'll be the jail for ourselves now, if no waur."

But Tackety was still full of fiddle music. "Hoch, it's a haet, man. We'll have Bailie Rose on our side seeing it was that Jock o' his was the cause o' everything. Aye and more than one in the Town Council, I'm thinking, for many were sweir to see a braw fiddler put behind bars.

"In the last resort I would make appeal to the Provost, who is a man, they say, that loves a tune. Maybe he'd pay Jamesie's debt, out of the Common Good if not out of his pocket.

"Come away to your bed. There'll be none of this the morn's morn. But when did we ever have such a jail dancing?"

The Course of True Love

YOUNG CAPTAIN WALCOAT stretched the fingers of his right hand — he was no great penman — and looked over the last words he had written. "I have read and reread my darling's tender words to me." He dotted the i, and reflected that this was one of his finest letters. What a lucky thing the other officers had gone off to the cockfight at Campbeltown, leaving him alone to this task. Only his scarlet jacket, belt and bandoleer, lying upon a chair, were in the mess to witness what he did, and they were in the secret. His gaze went out of the window: how lucky it was, too, that Fort George should have been thus planted out on the promontory, so that one could look past Ardersier Bay and up the Firth to where, its pall of smoke above it, lay the town of Inverness.

The sea was bright, the sky was bright, all the world was bright. For under that pall of smoke lived the source of all brightness. — O quick, let him get THAT down in his letter!

Who would have said, at the time he packed his bags in London to leave with his regiment for the barbarous North, that he should scarcely have unpacked them before he met his fate? So unexpected it had been, yet so inevitable. Someone had told him of the ball in Inverness Castle the evening he arrived. Tousled and stiff from the voyage, he had said he would not go. But they had hustled him off to it. And there, during the second dance, he had seen HER.

There she was, tendrils of brown hair straying, tilted nose, dimple in one cheek. It was as if he had known her always. More wonderful yet, it had been love at first sight for her too. He sighed, as one sighs with relief after a victory, and he took up his pen with renewed ardour. "My dearest girl, my own love ..."

They had had time for several meetings after that first momentous one: one in Provost Hossack's house; one by chance in the shops; one, the longest and most enthralling period alone together, walking about the islands of the River Ness. There had been only a plank for a bridge between one and another, and he had had to carry her delicious little person that trembled with fear, real or feigned.

He wished he were one of the seagulls circling above the sea, free to fly westwards to the town. Good! With slow care he wrote that in. "If I were a bird, and you were a bird, we would fly away together. I crave to be united to my dearest girl. The heart that beats in my bosom is not mine but my dear Betty's."

O yes, one of his very best letters.

But he had not signed his burning protestations before a cold thought struck him. What would his parents say to a match like this? They must hope, as so lately he had hoped himself, that he would let his regard light upon a lady connected with the Army, the daughter of some general – a colonel at least. The alliance would pave the way for a career of high distinction, together, of course, with an elegant establishment, a carriage and a fortune. Instead of which, he had fallen in love with a Highland girl, daughter of a merchant burgh. For that was what she was. Though her father was the Town Clerk and conscious of his station, his brothers, cousins, all his numerous connection, were happily and prosperously engaged in trade. Linen cloth, timber, herring and salmon they collected and shipped to London in their own or in others' ships. They had no dealings whatsoever with the Army, preferring peace to war in order to ply their trade. Their politics moreover were something mixed: though they were outwardly loyal to the Government, who should say what thoughts hid in the depths of their devious hearts? They would have been thorough Jacobites had it been expedient for them.

Betty was good and honest and sweet. Only she was not what his family would expect for him.

When he had added the scarcely necessary postscript, "I love you," he folded the sheet and addressed it on the outside to the Town Clerk's House, The Castle Hill, Inverness. He felt inclined for a stroll, and decided to take his letter to the post himself. Donning his uniform, he walked to the little sprawling village of Campbeltown. There were cream-white roses with small fine leaves of a bitter-sweet fragrance growing along the sandy track. He broke off a cluster to wear, then bethought him it would betray his lovesick state to his ribald friends, and threw the flowers away.

He would give his letter in at the office, taking care not to advertise the transaction. One must be prudent. The postman who plied between Campbeltown and Inverness was waiting there: the postmaster himself, Mr Francis Knowles, had not yet arrived. When he did arrive, Walcoat handed over his letter, first turning aside to kiss the place where he had written her name, Miss Betty Fraser. As he did so, Mr Knowles delicately coughed. He was a pleasant fellow, friendly to the English militia, which some were not, and Walcoat felt further drawn to him because he was a citizen of Inverness, that favoured town, and had the soft clear speech which Betty herself had. Today he was more friendly than ever.

"Is it yourself that's in it then, Captain? Fine day. The gentlemen are having great sport with the cockerels. You are not fond of the sport yourself, sir?"

"O yes, by Jupiter. I'm going on there now."

"Campbeltown is a small poor place, not like Inverness at all. You will be knowing that town well, Captain?"

Young Walcoat thought it wisest to disown any special knowledge. "Not well. I was stationed there a few weeks before coming here."

"You will not be knowing the Schevizes, father and son, who are in the linen trade?"

Walcoat answered, "No. What of them?"

"O, only that they have cloth of a fine quality. Many of your young military friends have shirts made from it. I wonder whether you yourself order from them?"

The Captain again answered, "No." He thought it a little odd that the postmaster should mention strangers to him: doubtless he had an interest himself in their linen trade. He did not attend much to it, lost in a happy dream of how Betty's blue eyes would light up at sight of his letter.

But Betty, if she radiated brightness, did not herself look in the least bright. She sat in a window nook in her father's house on the Castle Hill, bent over her embroidery, a puzzle and a trial to her mother.

What ailed the girl? She had been unconscionably homesick at her school in Edinburgh, and had been pleased to be brought home. She had scampered gaily about the house with her younger sisters. When she walked abroad through the streets she had looked so happy that folk had stopped and turned to look after her and murmured gentle things in English or in Gaelic. She had thrown herself into the social life of the town, attending with her mother the more innocuous of the card parties, the little balls and dinners at the houses of bailies and other burghers of worth. Her cousin William Schevize was said to have fallen as deeply in love with her as a young man so occupied in accounting could do. Her eyes had shone when she received her invitation as eldest daughter of the Town Clerk to attend the Garrison Ball.

Now even an invitation to another such had not lifted her from her heaviness of spirit. There she sat sighing, as from ennuie. Such a pity she was too old now to go with Mollie and Sybilla to the Ladies' Academy opened last year with a grant from the Town Council. — Or if only a ship from London might come in at Muirtown Wharf with a package from her brother Thomas, some fashionable thing, an Indian shawl, a new design in bonnets, a magazine.

How she pouted over that sampler! She was undoing stitches made in error. She had made the text run, "Who shall find a virtuous woman? HIS price is above rubies." Her father had laughed over it. But that was because he had been put into a high good humour by the success of his cousin Schevize's venture, in which he had an interest. He was not always so complacent, indeed he could be quite terrible to anyone opposing him — even to the Provost, it was said.

Betty had given up her embroidery altogether, and sat dreamily gazing out of the window, watching the gulls swoop and dive above the river. She would go out walking readily, that was something, with mother or sisters or with Isabella Hossack. She loved a fine prospect above all, and would stand stockstill upon the crown of the hill from which one could look west to Loch Ness and east as far as Fortrose and Ardersier. Hers was the age when girls become poetical.

Well! This ennuie she suffered at present was natural enough in her age: a young girl marriageable yet still unattached. Better for her perhaps to be quiet and sit at a window than to be running all the time to Garrison Balls like Isabella, or seek like some to stravaig the streets with the young officers who were ready for the company of pretty girls, when they were not taking their pleasure drinking in the taverns, playing at whisk for money with the resultant brawls that disturbed the town. Betty must never marry one of such a kidney, but some solid worthy comfortable merchant, such as ... well, her cousin William Schevize.

As soon as her mother was gone, Betty threw down her sampler and went on tiptoe in the opposite direction, to the door of the anteroom to the Town Clerk's office. She knocked very lightly upon the stout door, a special rhythm, and in a moment the door swung weightily open and there stood her father's clerk Alan Mackintosh, smiling. He had his pen behind his ear, smudges of ink upon his forehead and fingers, and his eyes with long copying of letters were bleared. Still he smiled, looking down on her from his great gangling height, and murmured tenderly, "Well, Betty!"

She took his cleaner hand and pulled him back into the anteroom, pausing with significant look towards the Town Clerk's door. "My father is not in?"

"He is gone out, consulting with the Dean of Guild anent the houses in Shore Street which have fallen into a ruinous condition owing to ..."

She reached up and put her hand without ceremony over his mouth, at which he nearly swooned.

For the truth is, if he had been able to formulate the thought, the poor fellow was head over heels in love with her. Yet from any declaration of the fact, either to himself or to her, he was debarred. And why? He was a cousin of hers on her mother's side: some remote but ungainsayable degree of consanguinity. Moreover, his mother had come, after his father's untimely death on Culloden Field, to settle in the household in order to suckle the infant Betty. He was therefore, in the romantic nonsensical old Highland way of thinking, Betty's foster brother. A bond as real as that of blood had from those early days united them but forbade them to marry.

Cared for and educated by the Town Clerk, he had exchanged a life of hard labour in the open air for a life of tedious labour among ledgers and books in a dim light in a close room. His only excursions were the Town Clerk's errands, meeting visitors, sending off visitors, supervising the packing and unpacking of goods at Muirtown, taking letters to and from the post office in Church Street.

He was the Town Clerk's clerk. He was Miss Betty's clerk too.

He was, indeed, her abject slave, and would do anything she bade him, asking no reward but the happy look on her dear little face. She wheedled and bullied him, and made him her confidant in the way that girls younger than herself made their dolls. Of this latest development of her life, radiant and terrible, she had told nobody but him. He was privy to it all: from the time when the messenger in uniform had come with an invitation folded in the shape of a cocked hat, to her dressing in a white muslin gown sprigged with tiny clusters of pink roses — it had come from London, worn by her sister-in-law but fresh as if new — to the moment when first she had realised the glories of Captain Walcoat (which Alan himself might possibly have missed) and had felt that extraordinary floating sensation. "I cannot truly describe to you the feeling, dear Alan," she said. "There is nothing I have felt before that I could compare with it. I despair of making you understand." Poor Alan understood only too well.

Captain Walcoat had danced with her in a polka and booked immediately for the waltz. She learnt that his first name was Adrian, such music. When it came to the minuet they had managed to steal away whilst Mamma was sitting on the front of her chair talking gossip with Mistress Hossack and the Dean of Guild's wife. They had stolen out on to the courtyard of the Castle hand in hand and looked down on the town lying beneath with its lit windows and dark streets and the wide swift gleaming river. They had looked up at the stars — Adrian knew much about them, having learnt on a campaign — till, as if bewitched, they were looking into each other's eyes instead.

Even by day, and Adrian engaged upon his tiresome duties, it was a transfigured town. Each street, each narrow vennel, was a way of

Paradise, for at the end of any HE might appear, striding in his scarlet uniform, gallant, heroic, legendary. One both feared and longed to enter a friend's house, for in any of them one might hear that deep vibrating voice and intriguing English speech. Any time, anywhere ...

Their secret meetings were sweetest of all. Once she had led him to the islands in the river under the pretext that they should see what were to be purchased by the town as a pleasure garden, and he had carried her from one to the other ...

But cruel fate ... stupid commander ... odious Fort George! Adrian had been transferred there, for an unspecified period, and he had had to go. The town had fallen into its old dull humdrum guise again.

The one joy was letters. Thank heaven for the postal system! Betty might write to her lover and he to her, even if they had to observe some cunning to keep their letters secret. This was the plan they had made: she did not address her letters in her round schoolgirlish hand, Alan addressed them for her in his neat clerkly one. And Alan, who went almost daily to the post office, Alan was able to receive any private letter for her among those of her father's, and convey it safe to her bosom. She would beam on him as reward so that his whole being was warmed, every loyal vein of him.

But now, alas! for many days his return from the post office had gone unrewarded, punished indeed by her sad and disappointed looks.

Now, as she pulled him into the room and shut the door, he was terrified by her angry face. "Alan, you are playing me false. You are not sending away my letters."

"O indeed, Betty! I have sent away every one."

"How then do I get no reply? I have had no letter in three weeks though I have writ twice or thrice. I think you throw away my letters, Alan. You do not want Adrian to receive them. Or else you are withholding his letters to me. You do not wish to see our affair prosper."

The poor fellow had not a word to say, he could only gape. Was ever devoted servant so unjustly used? There he was, serving her in a correspondence the discovery of which might earn her bread and water, but him no further bread at all! O but more, much more. For her sake he served the very man who would take her out of the house and out of his sight for ever. The only comfort was, if marry she must, she were better to marry the dashing captain than that grave calculating one they destined her for. Still, it gave him pain which he could not allow to himself much less reveal to her.

She was sorry, however, at the harshness of her words and with the quick melting that was so endearing in her she made amends. "Forgive me, Alan. I am so sad I say what I do not mean. I know you are true and send away my letters. But do you address them properly? Do they reach him? What if they should be opened and returned to me and my father discover ..." Her sudden pallor spoke for her. "Let me see how you address them," she went on. "O but I have seen. Why then does he not reply to me? Why does he keep this cruel silence? O Alan, believe me, I would rather you were in the wrong than he!"

She fumbled in the bosom of her dress and brought out a little silk purse. She had netted one like it for him once, to cheer him in an illness. It was the dearest thing he owned, too good for use. He would never receive another: now she netted purses for Captain Walcoat. "Here, Alan. Take this crown. Never mind if there is an extra fee to pay, do not haggle. But bring me back a letter. O Alan, please to bring me back a letter."

Many clerks of the town lived through the day for the trip in the evening to the post office. But Alan disliked it above all. His was a quiet nature; he abhorred the press of merchants and merchants' clerks who besieged the door of Mr Warrand's house-cum-office before a mail was due in. Some said the town of Inverness was unique in this, that while in other burghs the lieges waited calmly until such time as the horn blew to advertise the readiness of the post office to give out mail or until such time as a letter carrier might come to their doors with it, here it had become the practice for men to come personally, or by proxy, far ahead of the expected time. They had good reason for the practice! For the postmaster, Mr Warrand, was notorious for his cunning and irregular ways. He might give your letter to another to hand over to you, thereby putting you perhaps to the expense of standing him a bottle of wine over and above the fee. Worse still, he might give your letter into the hands of Margaret Robertson, the female letter carrier, who would most certainly not part with your letter from the inside of her greasy gown until you had paid twice or thrice the proper sum.

It was as much the chicanery as the din that afflicted the honest Alan. But it was part of his duty to come and receive on behalf of the Town Clerk, and it had become his privilege in the bygoing to receive on behalf of Miss Betty too. So now he waited patiently outside the building on the west side of Church Street. Some mail had come in: there were the steaming horses being led away. Since this was not a day for mail from Edinburgh and the south, there was a chance it might be from Nairn and Ardersier. When the horn blew, however, he did not go immediately in, but let the rest push their way through the doorway and wrestle for the attention of the postmaster and his wife. He turned to speak with Tobias Grant the Ardersier postman.

Grant jerked his head in the direction of the post office. "The old fox is in. He has taken time from his shipping to see to his public duties."

Alan replied, "I would sooner it were his servant."

"O no, do not say so! That servant of his, I found him two days since sitting with his feet upon the counter, reading out from a letter some young lass's sweetheart had writ to her to the two women servants, to make their diversion on it."

"He had opened the letter?"

"How else might he read what was within? He put a wax seal over the severed wafer, and the young lass would be none the wiser."

Alan said nothing, but some agitation arising from these words made him desire to get his business done with no more delay. He therefore pushed his way past those coming out, their letters in their hands. The post office was clear of crowds now. There behind the counter stood the postmaster Mr Warrand, burly of frame, florid of countenance. He was turning over and scanning the few letters not yet called for. He returned Alan's greeting with civility, for even the clerk of a Town Clerk commands respect, and immediately called over his shoulder, "Are you within, Helen? Are there letters from the east for the Town Clerk today? Here is his young man."

Behind him was the door into the domestic part of the house; a
most enticing smell of toasted cheese came from it. After a pause a
lady came bustling in. Alan had seen Mistress Warrand before, but
had never paid much attention to her — which was remiss, for her
family connection entitled her to some honour. She was the
daughter of the previous postmaster, Mr McCulloch. Upon his
death the office devolved upon her. It was through his marriage that
Warrand had become postmaster: like the throne of Scotland it had
come wi' a lass. They ruled now together.

"There are three letters," said Mistress Warrand, "from Nairn."
And she laid them upon the counter. "Four shillings and three
pence to pay, if you please." She counted over the money Alan gave
her.

Alan glanced down on the letters. One bore the crest of Nairn; it
was from the Provost there. The handwriting on the other two he
knew for that of business associates of his master.

"They are paid for!" Mr Warrand said, as if in surprise, "Why do
you not take them away? Please to close the door after you."

"But," Alan said, and it was as if Betty's heart fluttered within his
coat, "Are these all for the Town Clerk's family? Is there no more?"

Mr Warrand answered, "No." Mistress Warrand in the same
breath answered, "There is one."

Husband and wife then turned and looked at each other. All the
world knew they were a loving pair — had not the postmaster called
his new ship "The Charming Helen"? So now it was with mildness
that he protested, "My love, you are in error, I think. I have no letter
to hand over to this young gentleman."

And in the same breath and as mildly Mistress Warrand said to
Alan, "There was a letter for Miss Betty Fraser. It has been handed
to a friend of hers."

The young man remonstrated. "I do not think she would approve
of that."

But the postmistress added, with an ingratiating smile, "To a
close friend."

Mr Warrand then spoke more brusquely. "There is no letter here
for the Town Clerk's family. If you so wish you may search the
premises." Himself made a sort of search with his eyes, under the

counter, in a half open drawer, smiling all over his florid face, "You see there is none." Then, leaning forward over the counter, he said with a droll air, "Is somebody expecting one?"

Alan feared to speak further of it lest he rouse suspicion. "It is my duty to ask, Master Warrand. I am accountable to my master for the conduct of his affairs."

Mr Warrand bowed low, as if in admiration of such excellent sentiments. Mistress Warrand, from behind him, gave the hint of a curtsey in farewell. Only, as he closed the door after him, Alan thought he heard stifled laughter from the pair.

So, no letter for Betty today either. He must return her money to her silk purse and bring sorrow to her heart. "At least," he consoled himself, "if there is no letter, there is no room for mockery. What if it had been some letter to Betty that that servant opened and read to the maids? If it were her name they made sport of?" He began to think in Gaelic, imagining what he would do to any who so profaned his divinity.

It was high time that postmaster was deprived of his office!

Betty, when he put this aspect of the case before her, found no comfort at all in it. "I had rather them open and laugh over it than have no letter. What do you think, Alan? What has happened to make him neglect me? There must be some lady he has fallen in love with, prettier and more agreeable than I am — though who would have said he could find one in Campbeltown?"

"Well!" she would say, coming from time to time to the Town Clerk's anteroom and brushing aside the documents, wet or dry, strewn over Alan's table, "It is nothing to me. I do not care about it. I can forget him too." Then suddenly she would break out weeping and run to him, "O Alan!" And he would dry her face with his kerchief as carefully as he dried letters to the Lord Provost of Edinburgh.

Next day she came to him with a letter folded, ready to be addressed. "Ah, Alan, even if you loved me, here is a letter you would be glad to send to someone else for me." She had to explain herself. "In it I break with him, since he no longer loves me, he is free of obligation to me. Let him marry whom he will. I was in error to let my fancy go out after him. He is not worthy of me. I may be young and unused to a wide circle, yet I am the daughter of the Town Clerk of this burgh. I know my worth."

He had his kerchief half pulled out, but it was not needed. It was anger not grief this time. She watched dry-eyed as he wrote the address upon her letter: "Captain Adrian Walcoat, at the Fort of St George, Ardersier."

If the Firth waters danced as brightly as ever about the stout walls of Fort George, Captain Adrian Walcoat was oblivious of it. He was sunk in alarm and despondency. His heart had leaped up when, on calling at the tiny post office, he had found a letter awaiting him and recognised Alan's clerkly hand. Willingly he had fished out the required shilling — he would have given all he possessed for it. He had come back to barracks as if on wings, and run up to his room and thrown off his jacket and belt, the better to enjoy his darling's letter. And what had he seen? The dear scrawl upbraided him, attacked him, wounded him. Why? Why? After those splendid letters! What had he said in them to displease her? His love had been as warm and its expression as felicitous as he could imagine. They should greatly have pleased her. Yet here it was, in her own handwriting, though with more smudges and blots than he had ever known her page. "I can forget you too. Do not think you are my only suitor. I can console myself." The next word was quite blurred. Heaven above, what had happened? Was Betty out of her mind?

The young man groaned, laying his handsome head upon his arm. What could he say? What could he write to her? She was going to give him up for another, though they were as one flesh. The matter was urgent, and no post went out till tomorrow. Besides, he had not the wit to write with the force which the situation needed. Only if he saw her, he was sure, if he had as allies the tone of his voice, his speaking looks, the tender pressure of his hand, only then could he prevail with her. He must see her. He must go and see her.

He asked for leave on compassionate grounds, and his colonel could not withold it from a young man with so distraught a face. Next day he was on his way, riding the ten miles westwards along the shore of the Firth, beguiled out of his heaviness a little by the pleasure of the journey. But when he entered the town by the East

Gate and rode along the High Street among the refuse and horse
dung — the cleansing of the streets was still a dream in the Town
Council's mind — and when someone spoke to him in the Erse
tongue, then he felt strange and at a disadvantage. It was in this
spirit, when he had seen his horse stabled and procured a lodging for
himself, that he went up to the Castle Hill and presented himself
before the door of Mr Fraser the Town Clerk.

Here he had to knock three times before it was opened, an
unusual negligence. And when it was opened, it was by a
maidservant who exclaimed in Erse and made great round eyes at
sight of him. To his query, "Is Miss Betty at home?" Joanne opened
her eyes still wider and her mouth as well.

"La, sir!" she said, wringing her apron in her hand, "She is
indeed at home. But ... my master and mistress are at home too."

"Good," said the young fellow, to whom secrecy was not a
familiar practice. "Then be so kind as to ask them if I might have
some converse with their daughter."

At which Joanne wrung her apron the more, and began to make a
noise like keening. She shut the door after him, but seemed in no
mind to conduct him up the steep stairs to the hall within.

When he asked her to do so, she went backwards before him,
never taking her eyes off him, providing this strange convoy all the
way to the Town Clerk's room.

In his progress he could not be unaware of unusual sounds.
Mistress Fraser, in some other part of the house, seemed to be in the
hysteric passion.

Just as he was about to tap on the door, it opened, and out came a
burly florid person, who all but collided with the captain, to whom
he made profuse apologies — before stopping short and leering at
him in a most knowing way.

With the same opening of the door, Captain Walcoat went in. The
room was pleasant and dignified, a hearty log fire sent flickers of
light over the polished panelling, the portraits of the Lord Provost of
three years back and of Mr Fraser's mother stared down benignly
enough. Only it held some impalpable terror, so that the young
soldier, bold as he could be in a crisis, felt his heart beat rapidly.

The Town Clerk was not tall, but straight and well set up,

carrying an unmistakable authority. His visitor looked at him in instinctive apprehension. He gave his name, "May I recall to your remembrance, sir, Captain Adrian Walcoat? Lately of the garrison here, now of Fort George."

The Town Clerk blinked. "Walcoat? Captain Walcoat?" The two men stared at one another. Then it was as if the Town Clerk awoke out of a dream: "WALCOAT?" His voice went out in a roar, "Captain Walcoat, from Fort George? The devil take it, sir, you have courage for anything! I was about to seek a warrant for your arrest, and you walk in as bold as brass!"

"If you will inform me, sir, in what I may have given offence?" The young man tried to speak in his own great voice, but faltered.

"Here, sir, see here! Do you recognise these letters? Is this your writing, sir? Are these your sentiments? 'If I were a bird, and you were a bird, we would fly away together'! 'The heart that beats in my bosom is not mine but my dear Betty's' ... Is it indeed now? Are these letters which you have writ secretly to my daughter?"

He thumped with the back of his hand on several papers lying open and exposed upon his table. The young man did not have to step forward to see, indeed his legs at that moment might not have taken him. He put his head up, as if about to charge in battle, and said, "What if they are, sir? All that is amiss about them is they were sent somewhat secretly. There is nothing in them to give offence, such that your daughter should have felt herself obliged to reveal them to you." At the recollection of Betty's falseness, on top of her bitter words, he seemed to lose all fortitude altogether.

The Town Clerk gave a snort of laughter. "Is it Betty reveal them? Oho! Not she. I came by them after another fashion; 'pon my word, sir, after another fashion."

At which point the captain's eye fell upon the clerk Alan Mackintosh, who had returned to the room and whose dismal face might indeed have raised, in one who did not know the nobility of his nature, suspicions of the worst kind. "You!" he said, "It was you, and she bade me trust you!"

"Aye could she trust him, better than I can myself," the Town Clerk put in. "Well, he can go seeking now for another master to trust him."

"It's the postmaster, Captain," Alan answered the question still in the air. "It's that ... that obnoxious Mr Warrand. Some fellow in Fort George or Campbeltown became wise to the scheme, and sent word to Warrand to intercept any letters addressed to Miss here. He is just after being here and has put the letters into her father's hands."

"The swine!" Captain Walcoat said through his teeth, "The outrageous swine." Then, to the Town Clerk, "And you, sir, do not you despise the manner in which you are come by this knowledge?"

"Heaven send me patience!" the Town Clerk said with a terrifying grimace. "Do you stand there questioning the discovery before I have had time to question the offence?"

"The offence?" The young fellow's face grew red as his uniform. "Did I hear you say the *offence*? I have told you already there is none. Please to take the word back, sir. Do not let me understand you to have said the *offence*."

"Are you asking me to eat my words, puppy?"

"You are safe, sir. Your age protects you. Find someone younger, pray, to use the same term to me, sir, and I'll call him out, sir."

The Town Clerk was white as the other was red. "I have a son, sir. He is in London, but he can be recalled. I wager he will not hesitate to engage you."

But at this moment the door swung open and in rushed Mistress Fraser. Whether the high words of the gentlemen had reached her sanctum or whether she had seen fit to lessen the distance between herself and them, who shall say? Now, hysterics forgotten, in plain honest maternal anxiety she clung about her husband. "O not a duel, Mr Fraser! You must not risk our son. You know he cannot fight, and this is a soldier. Tom would instantly be killed."

"O pshaw, my dear!" returned the Town Clerk, "It is only a manner of speaking."

While the married pair were thus striving to come to an understanding of each other, there was a flash of pale muslin gown, and Betty, with hair more straying than usual and her tiptilted nose quite red with weeping, rushed into the room and fell into the arms of her lover. "O Adrian, I have heard all. And I thought you untrue! Forgive me, O forgive me. That monster of a postmaster, he devoured my letters from you. And I longed for them, Adrian. I did so long for them."

Tears and smiles were all deliciously mixed up together. The young man's heart, though full still of apprehension, could not but give itself to present bliss.

When the Town Clerk started forward to come between them, his wife held him back. "Let them be. Why should they not marry? He is well-born; it is not so bad a match for Betty."

But the Town Clerk set her aside resolutely: "Maybe, but it is a bad match for trade. You know we look for her to marry my cousin's son, a fine steady sober hard-working ..." Turning then to the captain, "I give you leave to go, sir! We must ask you to quit our dwelling and not presume to visit here unless invited to do so. — Come back here, Miss! You do no good by clinging to him."

But the best laid schemes even of Town Clerks gang aft agley. Mr Fraser had reckoned without his town. The affair became known in no time, and popular feeling was all in favour of the young lovers, and so outspoken that it all but toppled the postmaster and mistress from off their joint throne. Angry crowds gathered in Church Street outside the office and cried for vengeance in two languages. In the eyes of all Invernesians Betty was as good as Mistress Walcoat already. What cousin's son could in decency marry her now? She was regarded with as much love and awe — well, almost — as the Highland chiefs some twenty years before. Even the humble clerk Alan, his part in the affair being known, was treated with a deference which would have turned the head of a less modest man.

The lovers were made man and wife in the Town Kirk, the Provost and Council attending in full panoply with mace-bearers and all, outdoing the militia, and so impressing the family of young Walcoat that they went home to the South to boast about the high connections of their daughter-in-law.

And though the Warrands for a few more years tyrannised over the lieges at the post office, their tricks affected Betty and her husband not at all, for living together in conjugal happiness they had no need to write letters.

A Work of Necessity

IT WAS ON the Friday that His Lordship arrived for the Court of Session. The rattle of his coach upon the cobblestones of the town brought the lieges out on to the streets. There he sat, upright and dignified though not tall, his two attendant clerks on either side of him, his menservants behind. Folk gazed for the most part in silence. The majesty of the Law is apt to produce a silence; even the least guilty have an uneasy feeling when they see a High Court judge passing along their streets.

He, for his part, looked at them with a face of faint amusement, almost of disdain. It was certainly more than thirty years since they had been in arms against their King: times were peaceful enough now. Still, by his Edinburgh standards, he found it a backward place. He always carried his creature comforts with him on this Northern Circuit, namely his own chef whom he had recruited in Paris while doing the Grand Tour.

Now, as he rattled along, he raised a languid arm to brush off particles of dried mud from his fine plum-coloured coat, the gesture serving at the same time as acknowledgement of the scattered cheering and doffing of bonnets which greeted them on their turning down into Bridge Street.

One man, however, was too busy to come out and watch the gentlemen go by. It was only briefly that Hugh Ross the tailor saw them passing his doorway; he had looked up for that moment, biting off a thread. Perhaps in any case he saw only suits of clothes. He may have dimly wondered what it felt like to fit out a man of His Lordship's eminence. And then the coach was by.

It was to none of the town's common alehouses that they were going, not even to The Horns, but to a select hostelry whence all other guests had been sent packing to make room for them. At the hostelry, you may be sure, all were agog to receive His Lordship. Mine host and his lady bustled to and fro, chivvying the maid and the boy. Was His Lordship's bed-chamber adequately warmed? They had given him the one over the kitchen to get the benefit of the great chimney; there was a pleasant peat fire in it too. Had the boy remembered the hot water? Were the towels clean? The sheets? The curtains about the bed? Had Tom remembered to set a block of wood under one of the legs of the writing-table?

In the kitchen of the hostelry they were every bit as agitated, making ready to receive His Lordship's cook. The tailor's wife, Johann, was one of the auxiliary helpers engaged for the period. She had been very busy and was still hot and red in the face with stooping to blow up the fires. She had scrubbed and scoured every single pot and kettle, and ranged them in order on the shelves. On the last visit a terrible scene had arisen when Monsieur took umbrage at the lack of preparedness, and hurled spoons and ladles on to the floor by way of amending matters. Now there was water ready boiling, vegetables scraped and diced, meat tenderising in salt, salmon cleaned and prepared, fowls and ducks and geese plucked and dressed for the oven. They had remembered even herbs, mint and parsley — though that was perhaps lost effort seeing that His Lordship's chef would have his own dried herbs with him.

This night His Lordship was to dine out, at the Provost's. Mr Hossack was even now pacing up and down inside the front room preparing his speech of welcome. It was tomorrow that the judge's chef would show his mettle in public. Then he, with native cooks assisting him, would enable His Lordship to return hospitality by inviting the Provost and Mistress Hossack, the baillies and merchants of the town, the ministers of religion, the surgeon and schoolmaster, to a fête-champêtre, which traditionally would be laid out, weather permitting, upon the largest of the islands in the River Ness. There the barbaric taste-buds would be regaled with rare and mysterious flavours, dishes of fricassee and ragout, trifles and flummeries.

Yet now in a corner of the kitchen Johann had set aside something of her own, a dish of small Kessock herring pickled in vinegar with nutmeg and cloves. Had not the great man himself, on a previous visit when she served him at table with a concoction from his cook, said in her ear, "Guidsakes, honest woman, tak this stuff away and give's a wheen mair o' thae wee sweet herring"? The memory brought an added flush to her face, she straightened herself up a moment to her stalwart height.

With that she heard the coach and the clatter of mine host's feet as he came rushing down the wooden stairs to bow to the judge. Johann took off her apron and smoothed her hair, hoping she might be chosen to carry up to his bedroom after a while His Lordship's favourite refreshments of oysters and sherry. She wondered if he would condescend, if not to inquire for her potted herring, at least to greet her as one from whom he had accepted ministrations before. And perhaps there was a slight softening of the awesome face. But if so, that was all. Johann left the gentlemen to their confabulation, which touched upon when His Lordship desired to have his robes and bands conveyed to the court house against the Sessions on Monday. There was talk also of the fête-champêtre, of whether the ushers at the Academy should be included in the invitation, and of what measures could be taken to shelter the company in the event of rain.

Next day, however, the sun shone over the crowd of official guests and unofficial onlookers gathered on the island. Eyes were dazzled less by the sun than by the elegance of the southron visitors. The two clerks were in sober coats of brown and olive green respectively. How confidently they bore themselves, certain of their good style! His Lordship was magnificent in the plum-coloured coat, with this time a waistcoat of silver brocade. You may be sure most of the town's tailors were there to get hints. Hugh Ross was too busy finishing off a gown for the Provost's third daughter to be one, but he sent his son Adam, who memorised every detail from the cut of the coat lapels to the number of buttons at the knees of the breeches.

Johann meanwhile, with the other servants, once she had helped in carrying sundry dishes to and fro, trudged home and betook herself exhausted to her bed, where with her tailor she lay in peace till the small hours of the night. Then they were awakened by a noise not altogether unfamiliar in any town. — Whereas the eatables had been paid for from His Lordship's purse, the drink had been supplied by the town, and that liberally. It was known His Lordship was not averse to a glass. Moreover, there were many toasts to be drunk. First of all to His Majesty, the Hanoverian, then to the judge, then to the Provost and Mistress Hossack, then to the Dean of Guild, then to the learned clerks, then to the chef whose prowess had so amazed them. On it went. What wonder that the party who returned to the select hostelry behaved in another fashion from that in which they had gone? The two clerks, their arms round each other, were singing a passionate duet from the opera. His Lordship walked straight enough, but on arrival on the threshold he insisted upon removing his buckled shoes and setting them outside the door. Arranging them to his fancy, he proceeded to seat himself on the step and from there to act as if he were on the Bench. He swore in the tethering-post to speak the truth, the whole truth and nothing but the truth, and committed the mounting-block for contempt. After a little resistance he was persuaded upstairs by the host, and tumbled into bed. His retinue betook themselves variously to room or closet. The French cook was on the whole the most affected of all, which was but natural considering the strain under which his nerves must have been. He was already in a sleep so profound that he did not stir when they laid him on the straw of the kitchen floor.

All this made some little stir and hubbub in the neighbourhood, but in an hour or so stillness prevailed.

What was it that again woke the folk lying in the little houses by the river? A strange sound, a hissing crackling sound and, as powerful a wakener as the sound, a strange smell, one that alerts the nostrils of a careful householder — the smell of burning. Johann and her husband were up on their elbows in no time. "A fire?" In a moment they had pulled on clothes and were out on the street. One of the watch ran by, crying, "Fire! Fire!" They followed him. There was a wavering glow upon the Ness waters, just where ...? It was never the hostelry!

But it was so. Flames were flying out of the side door and window, sparks were whirling in the night air. "The kitchen!" Johann gasped, with professional alarm. "It's in my kitchen!" She was afterwards to concur in the general opinion that Monsieur had risen in his sleep and kindled a fire where no hearth was to hold it. All they could think of at that moment was how to get water to the blaze.

Johann's goodman the tailor was among those worthy citizens who set themselves to form a chain of buckets down to the river's brink. Water passed from hand to hand and was thrown on the flames. The fire in kitchen and scullery was brought under control after a struggle. Mine host, with boy and maid assisting, cast furnishings and gear into the street in the hope that most would be returned to them. The judge's clerks, sober now, followed suit, gathering up the law books and carrying them into the yard a safe distance from the flying sparks.

The fire downstairs was brought under control, but alas, it had taken the stairs which, being of wood, went up in a lowe. More water was called for and passed in. It was at this point that one of the judge's servants stumbled over objects lying by the threshold and stooped and picked up a pair of handsome buckled shoes — His Lordship's shoes! He carried them out respectfully to escape singeing.

His Lordship's shoes — but His Lordship, where was he? The servant cried out, and his cry was taken up from mouth to mouth.

"Where is the judge?"

"Where is Lord Gardenstoun?"

Everyone paused in what he or she was doing to echo the question. He must be upstairs still. The dire realisation paralysed them all.

All but the stout Johann. She pushed her way through the crowd of irresolute people and battled her way up the burning stairs and into the bedroom above the kitchen. There, smouldering bed-curtains illumined the white and stricken face of a man sitting bolt upright in bed. His Lordship had omitted to remove his wig and replace it with his nightcap. It added little to his dignity for it sat askew over one eye. Apart from the wig he was naked as when he was born. The floor of the room was in flames.

It was the action of a moment for Johann to roll him in blankets and heave him up over her shoulder as she had done many a time with a bale of cloth in her husband's shop. Then, slowed by the weight, she once more braved the smoke and fire on the stairs and, stumbling, coughing, gasping, won to the foot, where many willing hands beat out the flames that had kindled on her skirt and on the blankets. Johann set her august protégé upon his feet, others supporting him until the surgeon, hastily summoned, had appeared to pronounce him not injured but merely dazed. He and his retinue were accommodated in neighbouring houses.

Next morning when he and his party awoke, one would have liked to report that humble thankfulness was the uppermost thought in their minds. But in His Lordship's case it was not long before another thought supervened. When the Provost called to ask after his health, he had to receive him in bed, the clothes drawn up to his chin. He had his wig and he had his buckled shoes, but every bit of the rest of his wearing apparel had gone in the fire. Of the plum-coloured coat, primrose and silver waistcoats and the black breeches there was left not a trace. A nice predicament for a Lord of Justiciary to find himself in, and he with the kirk to attend today and the Court of Session to preside over on Monday!

At his command his clerks made no mention of it to the Provost. He, no doubt, would have made great efforts to borrow from one of the gentlemen of the town a suit which might roughly fit His Lordship. But from the indignity of such a thing the judge's soul recoiled. He could not make public appearance in the clothes of another man. He could do nothing but lie in bed, in the belief that one cannot lose one's dignity so long as one is not seen.

But this was a respite, no solution. This was the dilemma he was in when Johann arrived to inquire how he did. She found her way to his room to see for herself. And, strange to relate, it was to this lowly woman that he confessed it. Johann saw the solution right away. His Lordship must have a suit of clothes made, instantly, clothes of his very own.

The difficulty as to who could make them she brushed aside. Her husband, of course. He would go round his brother tailors and from them collect the finest material they had. They would give the hours of the day and of the night, until together they should have fitted out His Lordship as grandly as before.

Ah, but there remained a difficulty. The day was Sabbath. The intrepid Johann prevailed upon His Lordship's clerks to go round and call upon each of the three manses in the town, to explain the delicate situation and ask for a dispensation. It was readily agreed by all three divines that the proposed labour came under the category of a work of necessity. One went so far as to claim it also as a work of mercy.

I am happy to relate that when his sartorial crisis was over, His Lordship did reflect that he owed Johann his life. He bestowed a pension on her, so that she and her tailor lived comfortably for the rest of their days. I am inclined to think, however, that sweeter than cash to the tailor was the memory of how they had made His Lordship's suit.

. . . slowed by the weight, she once more braved the smoke and fire . . .

The Little Shoemaker

THE LITTLE SHOEMAKER had found a lodging for himself and his wife Margaret in the house of a decent widow living in the Haugh. They could have done with a larger room, since they had the possessions of a lifetime to stow away in it, and one with a better view than the chimney pots of the opposite houses, but their landlady was kind and kept an eye to Margaret, on account of whose health they had had to settle in the town — a town still known for its bland and gentle air. The shoemaker felt free to go about and seek a work-room for himself, since it was at that time generally accepted that if a man does not work neither shall he eat.

Finding a place to work proved more difficult than finding a lodging. Of all the shoemakers and cobblers he visited not one would have him work with him unless as a prentice, and that went against the grain with a man of fifty-odd. Worse still, it seemed the owners of empty premises were in league with the shoemakers and cobblers; not one of those he found suitable was open to hire. Church Street, High Street, Bridge Street and their connecting vennels, in none could he find a room in which to set up his gear.

Not that the townsfolk were aloof or surly. On the contrary, there were many who were at pains to advise a stranger upon what he should see of the features of their royal burgh. He was courteously directed to the Chapel Yard for a browse among the tombstones, to the Fort built by Cromwell more than a hundred years before, and to the Castle sitting upon its eminence over the river, a little apprehensively maybe, as having been ruined and repaired and ruined time and time again.

The little shoemaker listened with only one half of his mind to the interesting facts and opinions so freely given. With the other half, wherever he went and in whatever company, he strove to discover a room where he could work. It was at the Castle, of all places, while his self-appointed guide was giving him a pithy character sketch of the Duke of Cumberland, that his eye lit upon a derelict area on the south, the quieter side.

"Here the Prince blew up the outer walls, and you cannot blame him seeing that ..."

"What's that room for?"

"That's the officers' mess. As I was saying, what was not blown up was carted away by — I could tell you who."

"Well, but the room under it?"

"Whatna room? That ruined cellar? Aye, as I was saying ..."

The little shoemaker plucked up courage to ask one and another of the soldiers and serving-folk he met about the place, and from their replies he came to the gratifying conclusion that the room, the cellar, was at that moment entirely unused.

The plan formed itself in the shoemaker's head as he walked home. The cellar was apt to his purpose, a little on the large side, and very dirty and neglected, but secluded enough for him not to cause irritation by the noise of his hammer and, though not under the eye of the general public, occupying a central enough position in the town. There was also the great commendation that he would work free of charge, for since he did not know whom to ask for permission, he did not know to whom to proffer rent.

It remained for him to brush out the dust that lay thick upon the still undamaged floor and the cobwebs that obscured the still fine mouldings round the ceiling, then to set up the gear of his trade. His landlady was glad to see his bench go, for it had crowded up her doorway, and watched him with approval as he went labouring away, his back bent under the weight.

The shoemaker installed his bench of an evening, in the gloaming. He waited until the following evening to carry in his stool, his last and hammer, and the old leather bag which held his awl and curved needles and knife and waxed thread. The third evening he carried in a roll of hides. It was great good fortune that he found nothing had been tampered with, for, though he had found a battered old door and put it on hinges, there was as yet no bar on it and anybody might have come in to steal.

Finding that it was a place strangely unwanted by anyone except himself and out of everyone's way, the shoemaker got busy on a pair of shoes he had shaped out before. He set up his bench near the one window, which, being without glass or shutter, let in both the chill of the spring air and an entrancing vista of the river, the men fishing in their cobles on it and the women getting up their buckets of water at its edge.

He worked all morning and forenoon alone, then took the air in the doorway as he ate his frugal noon meal of bannock and cheese. A soldier or two passed within his line of vision, two working men and a dignitary with a servant at his heels. The shoemaker cast down his eyes less from humility than from the prudent desire not to be seen.

But in the afternoon as he rose to stretch himself and to rewax his thread, he heard a voice outside his door and met the staring eyes of a young private.

"What are you about there, honest man?"

"I'm making a pair of shoes, sir," answered the shoemaker, whose rule it was to be respectful to any customer however young.

"Will I get to see them?" asked the soldier with matching respect.

"Come you in, sir, come you in." The shoemaker stood aside to let him enter, but the young man hung back.

"Na, na! It's ower chilly in there. Bring them out here, if you please now."

The shoemaker brought out the unfinished shoes, and the young fellow took them in his hands and turned them this way and that, admired the stitching, then measured them to his militarily shod feet.

"It's myself will be needing a pair," he confided. "For I've been bought out, and am soon to go home. They'd fit me grand, what say you? Will I put them on and see?" In the end he asked, "What would you be taking for them?"

The shoemaker mentioned a low price. "Because you are my first customer in this town," he said.

The young man went away, to run back at sunset with the money.

The shoemaker gave a last dicht to the shoes and delivered them into the eager hands.

It was as the boy said, the cellar was remarkably chilly. Either it was damp or else it stood in the way of the wind. The shoemaker stuffed the window with rags. But he had to keep either the door or the window open for the light, lamp oil being as yet beyond his purse. He told himself he must keep warm with working.

And indeed he soon found work enough to keep him warm. The young soldier, pleased with his shoes, told others about him. The shoemaker had three customers before the first week was out, another four the following week, not counting those who brought him shoes to mend. They came to door or window, whichever was open, and did their business; few troubled to come in. The shoemaker found himself under the necessity of working late, luckily, since it was summer, without the use of a lamp. His wife was impatient for his homecoming, but trade is trade.

By the end of summer the shoemaker had won himself a name in the garrison, even in the town — that is, among such of the lieges as were in need of shoes. It came to the ears of the cobblers and shoemakers. Those who had sent him from their premises now doffed their hats to him in the street; those who had offered him prentice jobs would have been glad to take him into partnership. "The Castle Cobbler" he was called, yet he put up no sign above the door, nor made any parade when having another pile of hides carried up the Castle Wynd.

"I mind my own business," he said to any who urged greater show upon him. "Those that want me will find me."

The shoemaker's work kept him late. When autumn came and the nights began to draw in, he had to get a lamp to hang above his bench. He could well afford oil now. He was not home most nights till after nine o'clock. Those whose business or pleasure took them out at that hour and saw the modest fellow going quietly home would never have dreamed that the Governor of the Castle had ordered a pair of topboots from him. His savings were growing; in November he said to his wife that, when spring came, whoever lived to see it, they would be able to purchase a little house of their own.

What is whispered in closets is apt to be heard from the rooftops. The shoemaker's thriving state filled his colleagues with admiration to the point of envy. Yet to any who questioned him on his affairs and his customers, the wise man made guarded answer. "I mind my own business," he would observe, and leave it to his questioners to take the hint.

But then came a night when no-one would have envied the shoemaker. He arrived home in a pitiful case. He stumbled over the threshold and fell into the arms of the women, half swooning. His cheeks were pale, his eyes starting from his head. They had to set him down by the fire and get a glass of brandy into him before he could bring out a word.

When he did, the story he had to tell! The brandy was needed for the two who heard it.

He had been sitting at his bench busily at work, fixing an upper to stitch, when he observed the lamp burn blue, the flame turn sideways as if in a draught from the door. Yet the door was fast. There was an added coldness to the air, so that his cheeks goosefleshed. Then — how can one speak of such a thing? — a ghostly form grew visible. It was a tall soldier, an officer to judge by his golden epaulets and the cocked hat which he carried under his left arm. In his right hand he held a sword drawn from its scabbard ready for use. Who shall express the haggardness of his face, or the heart-rending sighs with which his bosom rose and fell? Down the room he slowly paced, turned with military precision at the opposite wall, then ran to a corner where suddenly, his hat falling from under his arm, he thrust and parried the blows of some invisible foe. After a few moments he became still, and stood without moving, whether in triumph or despair. It was likely to be the latter, since his next move was to fall on his knees, working his head from side to side in extremity of grief. Then, rising, he came up the room to the door. The shoemaker shrank back in terror, feeling with his nerveless hand for his hammer with which to defend himself. But the unearthly visitant, without bestowing a single glance upon him, turned and paced slowly down the room to the wall, to fall to his swordplay in the corner. Three or four times — or was it times without number? — he performed the sequence of actions. Then he vanished.

The shoemaker heard his stool fall over on the floor as he leapt up and made for the door. His frantic shaking hands could scarce get it open. He hardly knew how he had made home of it, nor lived to tell the tale.

It was not long before others were telling it for him. The shoemaker's ghostly officer was the talk of the town.

"Is it the truth?" people asked him. To which he answered, "Come you with me and see." An invitation which was universally refused.

"You will not dare go back to your work-room after this?" That was the next question.

To the surprise of all, to the chagrin of some, the little shoemaker set off for the Castle just as before.

He would return from his day's work each evening almost always cheerful, though on some occasions very pale and quiet.

"You have seen him again then?"

"Aye have I."

"Are you no feared, man?"

The shoemaker could not say that he was.

"Can you no ask him then why it is he comes? What is it lies upon his soul? Who is he fighting? What is it grieves him? Can you no be brave and ask him?"

To which the shoemaker replied, "What call have I to ask him anything? He is minding his business and I am minding mine."

The Sagart

IT IS A DULL TOWN that is without a character or two — originals, freaks or whatever you may call them. The citizens of Inverness, some time about the third quarter of the eighteenth century, were gratified to find themselves possessed of one. He appeared with dramatic suddenness at the corner of two of the principal streets, a place of constant resort: no-one saw him come; they looked up and found him there, standing with hand upraised as if prophesying.

Those who had only English said he was speaking Gaelic, those with Gaelic said English and a peculiar English at that. He scarcely needed to be understood, as a matter of fact, it was edifying simply to see him.

He was dressed in a long black coat, very old-fashioned and much worn; his stockings were dark (though somewhat disturbed by holes), and he wore broken Highland shoes. It was not that these articles of clothing were strange when taken individually: taken together they suggested eerie things.

What was chiefly remarkable in his appearance, however, was his beard, his long thick bushy grey beard. It was a wonder the urchins did not nickname him Beardie and torment him with mockery: they were equal for it. But there was something venerable about him and they were aware of it. When a nickname was found for him it was an honourable one, he was called the Priest, or Sagart. His subsequent actions confirmed the justice of the name.

For this was the time when the old High Kirk had fallen into disrepair, and was deserted by its congregation until such time as the Provost and magistracy found funds to restore it. The people worshipped in the Gaelic Kirk, the minister and session of which extended a brotherly welcome, declaring themselves willing to hold service of a Sabbath afternoon, leaving the forenoon for their English speaking friends. The High Kirk then was deserted. Winds blew in at its doors; its roof let in the weather upon its floor. A melancholy place, made the more melancholy by its standing surrounded by gravestones. In this unchancy place the Sagart slept at night. Yes, he was followed one evening and seen to go in; the next day when he was away prophesying people went in and found his bed, a heap of straw set down in the pew nearest to the pulpit. The rational might say he showed good sense in getting as far as possible from the draughts of the door; the more imaginative nodded their heads and held it for a sign of surpassing piety, quoting a psalm which tells of the sparrow finding a nest upon the altar of God.

By day when he was not wandering the Sagart might be observed reclining on the long grass of the churchyard, his back against a gravestone. Now who but a godly man would have dared do such a thing?

The Sagart found his own lodging: his food he could not find. For that he had to rely upon the charity of the town. Offerings of cheese and bannocks, milk and meat, were from time to time left for him at the lych gate by kindly women, who waited, hid, at a safe distance to watch him come and carry it off. "Cratur!" they would murmur, "Cratur bochd!" It gave them not only the warm feeling of a good deed done but the further satisfaction of having a sacrifice accepted by a divinity.

It might fall out occasionally, on wet or stormy days, that the women did not stir out of their houses. After a week's inclement weather once it was noticed that the Sagart looked a little thin, a fact which much grieved his benefactresses. Still, in the main, one or other was sure to remember him.

The fact is, the townspeople grew very fond of their original, though it was an affection not untinged by awe. His presence sat in judgement upon more than one. To the young, with a taste for pranks, he seemed the all-seeing eye; to the rich old merchants he foreshadowed death, the end of all endeavour. People took care to speak well of him as they spoke well of the fairies.

He was altogether an enigma. Even supposing him to be wholly human, a premise which many doubted, the reason for his living his austere life was quite unknown. It became the most frequent topic of conversation, ousting the weather. Was he a man obsessed by guilt or crazed by grief? Boys declared he had been cruelly used by his lady, girls that she had gone untimely to her grave.

Not only the natives of the town but their relatives and friends coming on a visit enjoyed speculating about it. One need never be stuck for conversation with such good material on hand. He was one of the features of the town: when one had led one's guests to the Castle, and the Islands, and the Fort, and Queen Mary's house, and the hill shaped like an upturned boat, one rose to a climax in coming to the Sagart, by far the most interesting because the most human.

Public visitors to the town too shared an interest. "I hear you have a mysterious character abroad?" said the Provost of Aberdeen. Folk came expressly to see him. He was what in later days might be called a tourist attraction.

The Sagart lived for almost two years in the town, surviving temporary food shortages and constant poor housing. Most of the townsfolk were of the opinion he looked pretty well, though his clothes had fallen into a state of disrepair worse than the High Kirk's own. Then some of the gentlewomen began to find themselves offended by his state. The rents and tatters were too large and too numerous. He was hardly decent even for an ascetic. The Provost's daughters, home from boarding-school in Edinburgh, professed themselves shocked, and urged their father to have him sent forthwith to the outfitter's. This was, of course, out of the question. And the good Provost had many other things on his mind. He fobbed the young ladies off with promises. It was not until the Provost of Elgin, on an official visit, ventured to murmur in his ear that for a town of such importance as the capital of the Highlands their original was a little on the shabby side that he took any action. He placed the state of the Sagart's wearing apparel before the ministers of the town.

It was surely their business more than anybody's, not only because they were the known dispensers of charity but also because it was hoped they could from their own wardrobes provide clothing of a style suitable to the Sagart. It fell to the minister of the High Kirk, his involuntary host, to put up the main part of it. He was willing himself, kind soul, to sacrifice one of his two current suits of coat and breeches. It was his wife who prudently pointed out that his cast-off suit would do, in fact would do better. Poor Mr Macmillan rather liked his old suit, it being the one he wore when sitting at ease in his garden. But he obediently got it out of the chest.

His colleague of the Gaelic Kirk begged to be allowed to contribute his quota. He added hose, and a pair of thick-soled shoes that had many a day's wear in them still if they were changed from foot to foot.

It is well known that the heart is enlarged by giving, one cannot give enough once one has begun. The divines felt they could not do too much for the Sagart. They added a cloak with a lining almost intact. Then they bethought them of his head. This, they realised, was unprotected even by a blue bonnet, only his now scanty grey locks covered it from the stormy blast. What sort of headgear would go with the articles of clothing they were providing? — Surely nothing less than a cocked hat.

That raised a problem. Only a few of the leading citizens possessed one. Until a few years back indeed only three had, the Sheriff, the Provost and the Minister of the High Kirk. Mr Macmillan was having a battle with himself, striving to become willing to give up even his hat. But his wife, whom he consulted, was horrified. That was going beyond bounds, she said; it would be a temptation to the Sagart, making him puffed up with pride; it would, to permit the pun, go to his head. She made a counter suggestion, that she should cause to be fixed to the cloak a good warm hood of roughly the same material. This carried the day.

They waited until the Sagart was reported as taking a turn along the Ness. Then the whole set of clothes was rolled into a bundle and given to Mr Macmillan's man to carry. The fellow was very superstitious, and despite his master's chiding utterly refused to carry it further than the lych gate. It was Mr Macmillan himself who with his own hands bore it into the vacant echoing kirk and disposed of the articles in an attractive manner upon the pew as upon a bed. Even without the cocked hat it looked a generous donation.

You may imagine that the divines and those privy to their charitable action awaited with eager anticipation the appearance of the Sagart in his new guise. To their consternation he never appeared at all. Though they took their walk by the churchyard early the next morning, there was no original among the gravestones. When they went and peered in at the broken door, a bird flew out twittering over their heads, but there was no human person there. When they entered in and approached that front pew they found the clothes were gone. By the evening they had made enquiries of one and another, but no one at all could report having seen him at street corner or riverside.

Days went by and nights. Everyone began to ask, "Where is the Sagart?" To the dismay of all he was never anywhere to be seen. Weeks went by, months. It was clear he had vanished, old clothes, new clothes, everything. Only a wisp or two of straw blowing in the draughts in the High Kirk gave any hint that he had ever been.

His disappearance, happening immediately after the giving of the clothes, could not but be linked with it. The matter caused as much speculation as his presence had done before. Had he been displeased with the quality of the gift? — The minister of the Gaelic Kirk still thought of the withholding of that cocked hat. — Had the clothes been altogether too old? — Or too new? Too grand? Had Mistress Macmillan been right: raiment so good must surely put an original above his station? The Sagart must have resolved to be henceforward as other men.

The last and most popular view was that it had been a mistake to have given a gift at all. The giving of gifts in the Highlands has always been a tricky business: one has to go very delicately about it, else one may at the same time give dire offence. The Sagart might well have felt himself humiliated by the suggestion he was not decent, and been highly resentful of the patronage. Food he might accept; his clothes were his own affair. He was not, in local parlance, in the reverence of them. But why then had he taken the clothes away?

This was a new mystery, the new topic of conversation. But, with the hero himself absent, a melancholy one, one that had gradually to die away.

The Absence of Mr Clark

ON AN EVENING of June 1812 a dinner party was being held at the house of Provost Gilzean, a gala affair with sirloins and game, flummeries, trifles and blancmanges, not to speak of brandy, claret and port wine. It is necessary when you are Provost to entertain in a manner befitting the dignity of the town.

Most of the guests were town dignitaries, bailies, large merchants, local landowners and the like. But among their portly forms was a graceful slender one, that of Mr John Clark, assistant master in the Latin Class of the Academy. He was the favourite teacher of young Hector Gilzean: less of a distinction perhaps than might at first appear since on the whole that young gentleman did not care for teachers as a breed. It was on Hector's favour that Mr Clark's invitation to the Provost's dinner party rested. The boy sat next to his guest at table — it would be hard to decide which had the heartier appetite; and after dinner when the company settled, some to billiards, some to cards, he suggested that they might find better diversion beyond the confines of the house.

But before they could effect an escape, Mrs Gilzean bore down on Mr Clark, to shower compliments upon him. As well she might, for it had caused her maternal heart the greatest pleasure that at the prize-giving about to take place her son was to receive an award. For Latin too, a subject he had never shown much taste for while his instruction was in the hands of Mr Campbell, Principal Latin Master — "that old dragon" in Hector's playful phrase. How fortunate for the boy to have latterly had so kind, so compliant a master as this other! Hector positively enjoyed classes with him, coming home with many a lively anecdote with which Mr Clark had illustrated his lesson. What a surprise and what a pleasure that he among one hundred and six young gentlemen should carry off a Latin prize! Papa could scarcely credit it, Mamma was transported with delight.

Everybody knows that two o'clock in the morning is not a very comfortable hour for humankind. If one wakes then, one's thoughts tend to be very gloomy; worries appear doubly worrying. Mrs Gilzean had a worry, and that was that in October her beloved Hector was going to Aberdeen University. In daylight hours she did not think it much of a worry beyond saying to herself that she must mark all his linen. But at two a.m. the night after the party she woke and trembled at thought of the many dangers, physical and moral, which would surely surround him in that great city.

But the night hours sometimes bring counsel, and at three a.m. the fond mother had suddenly seen a way out: why should not young Mr Clark accompany her son as tutor? With what confidence would she entrust her darling to him.

In no time at all she was sitting up in bed and nudging her husband on the shoulder. He was Sheriff Substitute of the County as well as Provost of the town, no end of a bigwig, yet she nudged him as if he were any ordinary man in a night-cap.

"My love!" she said. "I have just conceived a wonderful idea. Why does not that nice Mr Clark accompany Hector to Aberdeen in the autumn?"

The Provost came up through layers of sleep and for some time could not gather his wits. But in the end he said rather shortly, "Because he cannot," and went to sleep again.

But as they dressed in the morning Mrs Gilzean returned to the attack. "I think Hector would mind him, he is quite under his influence. I must say, Provost, such an arrangement would greatly relieve my mind. '

"It is impossible, my dear. Be reasonable. Young Mr Clark is engaged to the Academy. He is Assistant Latin Master."

"I know it well. But surely for Hector's sake he could get leave?"

"My dear, he is needed for the boys. It would be prejudicial to the discipline of the school, of which, you are well aware, I am a director — in fact, Chairman of the directors. It would hardly do."

"Think how economical it would be. We should not have to pay the young man a salary, since he would be in receipt of the emolument given by the school."

The Provost was rather an indifferent Treasurer to the school, a fact not widely known since for some years now he had forgotten to have an audit of his books. Still, he had been a friend to it since its inception some years before, and he had the grace to shake his head.

"I am supposed to have the interest of the school at heart."

"Well, is not our son a pupil of the same? It is no great extension of his normal duty for Mr Clark to become his tutor."

The Provost sighed. "Well, I can but put it to him."

Mr Clark, when the suggestion was put to him, was taken with it. What else could he be? It is much easier to look after one young gentleman than one hundred and six. And it is very pleasant after being in a small town to go and live in a city.

The autumn term had begun at the Academy. Mr Adam the Rector was still immersed in the lists of names, timetables and the like which form the inevitable preoccupation of the first few days. But on the third day of term, upon coming out of his study, he found his ears assailed by the most untoward, the most deafening din. His first thought was that the noise emanated from outside the building, a riot or some public mourning or rejoicing connected with the War. Then to his astonishment and dismay he found it came from within. It came, indeed, from the hall where was the Latin Class.

Whatever could be afoot? Where was the excellent Principal Latin Master, Mr Campbell? If he were present, what had happened to him? Had he suddenly died? Had he — horrid to conceive of — been made away with?

The Rector's gown floated behind him as he went at speed to the scene.

Once there he stood aghast at what met his eyes. For there was Mr Campbell, the finest disciplinarian the school had known, pacing up and down as if at his wits' end, now threatening, now coaxing, a mob of boys. Some fought, rolling on the inkstained floor, some were throwing darts, others quieter but no less reprehensible lay on their stomachs playing at cards.

The presence of the Rector, as it gradually became known, quieted the din. Though not severe, though indeed of a mild temper, he was famed for his erudition and commanded respect on that account. There was a jumping back into seats, a smoothing down of jackets, a pulling out of books and scratching of pens. Darts and cards as if by magic disappeared.

Having addressed a few trenchant words to the young gentlemen, the Rector held a whispered conversation with his Latin Master. Mr Campbell's eyes were flashing with anger, his breathing unequal.

"Rector, it is impossible to keep discipline among so many with no assistant. The class is too large for one."

"Granted, granted," said the Rector in a conciliatory voice. "Where is Mr John Clark?"

"Where indeed! Mr Clark has never been here since term began."

"What do you say? Not been here?"

Mr Campbell's ire was in no way abated. "But did you not know, sir? Were you not made aware of his intention?"

"He spoke to me once when we met in the street, but only casually, I did not understand what he meant. I understood him to say that he felt it his duty at some time to go to the University of Aberdeen in order to complete his studies."

"His studies are already completed, sir. How could he have been taken on to our staff if he had not his Master's Degree?" He paused, then breathing with greater difficulty he said, "Mr Clark has gone to Aberdeen as tutor to young Gilzean. He has abandoned —" The angry master stopped before embarking on a figure of speech and added simply, "– his duties here in favour of a private undertaking. I confess to you, it is not only dereliction of duty but the matter of his salary which vexes me. Are you aware, Rector, that his salary is still being paid to him?"

Here the diplomatic Rector saw fit to terminate the conversation; saying, "Later, later, Mr Campbell!" he went out of the temporarily quiet room.

But the thought of the salary remained in his mind, and when he next met Mr Campbell it was his first topic. "Regarding the absence of Mr Clark, I take it very much amiss that he spoke to me only casually in the street. He ought to have asked leave of absence in writing. I could then have taken steps to appoint an assistant for you in his place. Indeed he might himself have supplied a substitute, until such time as he returns, yes and paid him out of his own pocket. For I agree with you, it seems monstrously unjust that a master should absent himself and at the same time receive emolument.''

"Precisely. In default of a substitute his salary should have been added to my own, since it is I who bear the burden and the heat of the day. To tell you the truth, Mr Adam, such an addition would but bring my salary up to the level at which it should by rights be. I have gone short all last session.''

The Rector sighed. "I too, my dear sir, I too. I find it a delicate subject to raise with our Treasurer, but it is most vexing to me that I should not have received the sum promised in writing at the time of my appointment.''

"And for how long, pray, is Mr Clark likely to be absent? What was said to you on that head?''

He looked so severe that secretly the Rector trembled. "Let me see, let me see. When I remonstrated with him — I recollect I did remonstrate — he said 'the father of his pupil would see to the matter'. Yes, that is what he said. He spoke so confidently I did not remonstrate further.''

"Then, Rector, you must seek out Provost Gilzean.''

"Yes,'' echoed the Rector, "I will seek out Provost Gilzean.''

Mr Adam did not relish the prospect of seeking out the Provost, either at his mansion or at the Court House, and he blessed his good fortune when it so happened they met face to face in the High Street. The Provost moreover was alone. He was most gracious, stopping and lifting his hat. "Well, well, well, Rector! A pleasure to see you out, sir, enjoying the invigorating air. Wonderful weather we are having for the time of year.''

He was about to pass on, but the wily Mr Adam asked a question which arrested him. "How is Hector doing in Aberdeen?''

"Splendidly, splendidly,'' the Provost beamed. He took a pinch of snuff. "Hector will do very well there. Sometimes a change of scene is all a young man needs to bring out latent powers — latent powers, sir. Yes, I think with a little application he will begin to make strides. He is, as you know, under the careful guidance of your Latin assistant master, Mr John Clark. A very accomplished fellow, Hector has taken greatly to him and will profit much by his influence."

"It is about Mr Clark that I should like to speak with you," returned the Rector, "While fully aware of Hector's needs, and indeed sympathetic towards them, I cannot disguise the fact that we are feeling Mr Clark's absence sadly at the Academy."

The Provost waved his hand. "But is it not all education, my dear Mr Adam? A young man meeting new experiences, a new world opening out to him, the world of men — is he not in need of some wise Mentor who shall protect his morals from contamination, lead him and — is not it all education?"

He seemed prepared to be moving on. "If you will forgive me, Rector. An important matter — arrangements for the Circuit."

Mr Adam realised he was speaking to the Sheriff Substitute of the County. All the same he was determined to pursue his objective. "One moment only, please, Provost Gilzean. I feel it is incumbent on me to state that the school is suffering grave loss from the absence of Mr Clark. I should be obliged if you would give me a firm date for his return. I trust it will be a speedy one."

The Provost was already some paces away. "Leave it to me, my dear sir. I will consult the directors. I will put the point before them. Good morning to you."

Things got worse rather than better in the Latin Class.

The Rector was therefore relieved to fall in with Provost Gilzean a week or two later. This time he was accompanied by Mrs Gilzean, so that the Rector had to spend more time asking for Hector. But as soon as courtesy was complied with, "Provost!" said he, "May I now know from you when Mr Clark is likely to return to us? Some while past you promised me —"

"Why yes, yes," answered the other. "I was about to inform you. The directors met and I mentioned Mr Clark to them. They are pleased to tell you they hope he will be resuming duties at the Academy —"

"When?"

"O let us say, in time for next session."

"Next session! But that is ten months hence. We cannot possibly allow Mr Campbell to supervise the studies of so many without assistance. Think, Provost! There are well over a hundred lads in the Latin Class."

The Provost sighed. His wife exhibited signs of ennuie, and he was plainly wishful of walking on with her. "Well, then, Mr Adam, shall we say next YEAR? It is after all but a few weeks until it is the New Year. Bless my soul, 1813! How the sands of life run! Let us hope we shall see victory and peace from all war."

"Then we may depend upon Mr Clark's returning in the New Year?"

The Christmas holidays came and went as swiftly as holidays will do. The school reassembled in bleak January. The uproar in the Latin Class was worse than ever.

But in February, with the earliest Spring flowers, came Mr Clark. He arrived one morning without prior notice, as mysteriously as a fairy. He was happy, pleasant, at ease and anxious to put everyone else at ease too. He looked well, and was more than ever well groomed and modish in his dress. He soon had his portion of the Latin Class as quiet as mice. There was no sound except from time to time a ripple of wholly legitimate laughter. The young gentlemen sat attentive in their places listening to his words. True, when the Rector paid the class a visit his ear detected references rather to the latest thing in boots than to the "pons asinorum". Still, there was no doubt the class was orderly enough.

If the Rector was pleased, we may hazard a guess that Mr Campbell saw his assistant's success with mixed feelings.

All was now outwardly well. But there was trouble below the surface. It so happened that a clergyman uncle of one of the boys invited him to construe a passage from Cicero. It should have been a pleasure to any Academy boy to do so, but the young man protested that he had not seen that speech before.

"Well, sir, never mind. Look it over and give me your translation."

Georgy was utterly tongue-tied.

His persevering uncle pulled out a volume of Caesar, stuff for the First Form surely, and tried him with that. The young gentleman, unhappily stumbling, was unable to construe one word in three.

His amazed uncle opened the eyes of his brother to the shocking fact that his son, now in the Fifth Form, was quite incredibly deficient in Latin. That gentleman in turn was shocked, and dismayed too. Questions put to Georgy and his friends confirmed him in his opinion that something was far wrong with the teaching of Latin in the school.

The matter weighed so heavily on his mind that he could not but mention it to a brother laird when they met at a cattle sale.

The spotlight must now rest upon this laird, Mr Mackintosh. Abounding in energy, mental and physical, he could never suffer an unsatisfactory state of things to exist. He had recently returned from business abroad, and now, released from responsibilities and filled to excess with love for his native land, he was positively on the lookout for some cause to fight on her behalf. Old pupil of the Academy as he was, he was the more interested.

He now took the step of visiting the Rector and declaring to him in no uncertain terms that the standard of Latin in the school left much to be desired.

It is said that a true joke is no joke. In much the same way a just complaint is more painful to bear than an unjust. The fact that the Rector knew the state of Latin to be deplorable added to his pain. The absence of Mr Clark had caused an absence of Latin, which his return had as yet not made good. He felt, as he afterwards confided to Mr Campbell, between Scylla and Charybdis.

But the criticism which he had so unjustly to bear was only one of his preoccupations. The other, exacerbated by the first, was his salary, the arrears of which had still not been paid. Mr Campbell smarted under a similar injustice, namely that the directors should have made over to him the salary of Mr Clark. The two grievances acted upon one another as stone and flint and a spark was kindled.

The Rector, leaving out the Chairman Provost Gilzean, wrote to one and another of the directors, complaining not only about Mr Clark's absence, but also of their failure to pay him, through their Treasurer, his just emolument.

The result of his action was that on a certain date in March he was called to a meeting of the directors of the Academy.

He went in high hope. As he rose that morning he rehearsed what he would say before that august body, the pleas he would make, not now privately but officially, cogently, impressively. He rehearsed some flowers of rhetoric and even a decorous joke or two, for it is known that a touch of pleasant wit helps on a man's cause. He took special pains with his dress, caring even for his shoes to be polished with greater thoroughness than before by his little servant.

He lost something of his elation, however, when he was kept waiting for half an hour in an anteroom. When at last he was shown into the chamber he was surprised to see that the attendance was small, only something over half of the directors were present. He was gratified to find that Provost Gilzean was not in the chair, ex-Provost Grant acting for him.

After scant ceremony Mr Grant spoke. His speech was brief and to the point almost of rudeness: the Rector must not give any information whatsoever about the Academy to any other director than to their Chairman Provost Gilzean.

The Rector burst out inadvisedly, "But he is the last person ..."

"Come, come, my dear sir! What more discreet and respectable person could you confide in?"

"It is only that ..."

Ex-Provost Grant pulled out his watch. "You will pardon us, if we tell you, Mr Adam, that we have other affairs to see to. Is it understood that you give no information to any director other than Provost Gilzean? Should you communicate with any other, whether by speech or writing, I must make it plain to you that we should have no recourse but to relieve you of your duties."

Mr Adam left the room as if stunned. He was almost at his own gate before he recovered his senses. A threat! That is what had just been made to him. A threat! He, the highly respected Rector of the Academy, had been threatened with dismissal as if he had been a mischievous errand boy. No Briton had been more humiliated since Boadicea.

So amazed was he that he scarcely noticed that Mr Clark had again absented himself. His thoughts were so loud within him that they drowned out the uproar in the Latin Class.

But there are few clouds without a silver lining. The Rector in his dark hour could not foresee the champion who should spring to his aid.

This was none other than the spokesman for the parents who had complained of the falling standard of Latin in the school, Mr Mackintosh. Meeting this gentleman by chance one Saturday the Rector could not help reverting to the painful subject, and by way of justifying himself he stated that the fault lay with an assistant master who, trifling with his duties at the beginning of the session, had now appeared to be abandoning them altogether, absenting himself without permission, even without the knowledge of his Principal. Once launched upon the theme the injured man went further than he had meant to go, and poured out to the attentive ear the story of his summons to the meeting of directors and the threat, yes the THREAT, made to him there.

The interest of his listener at first focused less on the insult to the Rector at the meeting than on the meeting itself. "I am a director myself," he exclaimed, "Yet this is the first I have heard of a meeting being convened." He went away frowning.

He found he had good reason to frown. After researches made, it became clear to him that to the meeting in question only the town directors had been called: the county directors, of which he was one, had been left out of it. The meeting therefore was a secret one, behind closed doors.

It was then that the full story burst upon his consciousness. He saw plainly the wrong done to the school, to the Rector and to his Latin Master, and he saw why that wrong had been glossed over, hushed up, and in whose favour it had been done. Someone in a high place was abusing his position, selfishly overriding the public interest for his private one. He boiled with indignation. He could brook a lack of justice worse than a lack of Latin. He took counsel with his fellow county directors, whose minds he inflamed; but the action decided upon was taken by himself alone.

Signing himself with a terrifying pseudonym, he wrote a trenchant letter to a local newspaper, telling the whole story of the absence of Mr Clark, and laying the blame for it plumb at the door of the Provost of the town.

Editors of newspapers have need of both valour and discretion.

The editor of this one felt he had more of the latter commodity: he was greatly adverse to publishing a letter which took the lid off so unsavoury a business. But Mr Mackintosh had valour for two, and his energy, plus the editor's own sense of justice, lent him the courage to publish the letter. Publish he did, thereby advancing in no small way the cause of free speech and democracy.

The letter was the talk of the town. The Chairman quickly called an open meeting of directors. — Too quickly, which was very clever of him. The date named was April 13th, a time dedicated by farmers to sowing, so that though duly apprised the county directors were unable to attend.

This fact was pointed out forcefully by the champion in a further letter. He left the Chairman of Directors not a leg to stand on. Nothing could be said to refute the charges made.

But the Provost kept a rod in pickle for the Rector.

Summer passed. The new session began at the Academy. And Mr Clark was found to be absent yet again. He had gone, with his pupil, to Aberdeen, this time "to study music." There was plenty of music in the Latin class.

It was not to be borne. The Rector went to see individual directors again, and complained to them in no uncertain terms. Whereupon he was summoned to a meeting of the Board. And was dismissed. Dismissed! How could he be, he whose terms of appointment were "ad vitam aut culpam"? Of what fault was he guilty? What charge had even been preferred against him? He refused to accept his dismissal. But, since his emolument ceased, dismissed he must consider himself to be.

And here, into a situation which he rightly described as "chaos and old night", rushed Mr Mackintosh. In no long time he had the Rector geared up to bringing his cause right up to the Court of Session. It roused the attention of the whole nation, dwarfing the Napoleonic War.

For there the Rector was vindicated by a unanimous judgement of five Law Lords. They pointed out that the directors were bound under charter to dismiss teachers only upon due cause shown, ("ad vitam aut culpam") and not at their own pleasure, that no due cause could be shown, since Mr Adam was universally recognised as an able teacher and a most respectable man. He had been dismissed without trial, even without accusation, a piece of injustice affecting the whole of the nation. When further it was declared that "no body of men in the kingdom are better entitled to protection than those who are employed in the education of youth" a timely blow was struck for the status of the teaching profession.

One might wonder whether Mr Clark himself in all this rumpus was represented only by his absence. His story, however, has a happy ending. Mr Campbell on leaving his post some years later recommended as his successor none other than Mr John Clark who "had given him great assistance and was all that a teacher should be". His absence therefore must be seen only as a passing peccadillo.

The Provost weathered the storm and was to prove useful to both town and school. As for the champion, Mr Mackintosh, he lived to fight other battles, an activity which he seems very much to have enjoyed.

A Dark Grey Coat

MR BISSET WAS session clerk to a church in a small town near Inverness. He was a landed gentleman; his was an affluent household and its members had reason to be happy. Indeed, on a certain Saturday afternoon in the year 1849 the only dismal person in the house was the master of it. He sat moodily before his desk, when he was not pacing up and down his study floor.

It was in his capacity as session clerk that Mr Bisset was troubled. Their Minister, the Rev. Arthur Chisholm, was away attending a Commission of Assembly in Edinburgh; and Mr Bisset, engaged all week upon his own business affairs, had that morning awakened to the fact that no "supply" seemed to have been arranged. How such a thing should have happened was beyond understanding. Mr Chisholm must have left the matter to him, and he to Mr Chisholm. His earnest endeavours to find a preacher in this and neighbouring villages had proved unavailing. There was no one to conduct divine service on the very next day!

No proper person, that is. He himself, as under-shepherd, must lead the flock in the pastor's absence. Well, it had fallen to his lot before. He had announced the psalms and read the Scripture portions: no difficulty in that. What had been difficult was the prayers; he had had secretly to read them, having taken the precaution of composing them beforehand. As for the sermon, that he had read quite openly from a published volume. One or two of the strictest had remarked unfavourably upon it.

Now it must happen again, and whether through his fault or that of Mr Chisholm ...

The study door was opened discreetly.

"What is it, Mary?"

"It's a visitor, please, sir. Asking for the master. He did not give his name, but said you would know him."

"Is he a hardship case?"

The girl looked shocked. "O no, sir! Nothing of that sort. A very respectable-looking person, in a dark grey coat."

"Well, show him in."

Mr Bisset rose to meet his visitor. A man in middle years, he was more than the girl had said: not respectable so much as distinguished-looking. His crossed cravat and his dark grey coat suggested, while not exactly proclaiming, a divine. Mr Bisset had a confused impression that he had once, on an august occasion, seen his face before.

"I beg a thousand pardons, sir," said the stranger in a deep melodious voice, "for having interrupted you in the midst of your ..."

Mr Bisset gave a deprecating flip to the papers on which he had been idly scribbling, but he felt flattered.

"My intention," the stranger went on, "was to call upon the Rev. Mr Chisholm."

"Mr Chisholm is not at home. He is away this full week in Edinburgh."

"So I found at the manse. I was for turning around and going home, but the lady of the house — his housekeeper? — suggested my calling upon you. And I was tempted to profit by my being in your neighbourhood to ... I believe you are session clerk? Yet, till now, I have not had the pleasure of speech with you."

He had a diffident way with him, which, in so distinguised a man, Mr Bisset found charming.

"I am glad that you did!" he replied. "Though I am sorry for your disappointment in not finding Himself at home. You had not made an assignation with him?"

"A long time ago. Too long to expect he should burden his memory ..."

A wild hope surged in the session clerk's breast. "You had made an arrangement with Mr Chisholm? I mean, to preach?"

A smile touched the attractive, rather melancholy face. "I thought only to visit him on this occasion. We are friends of long standing. Yes, for many years I have had the honour ... such an eminent scholar, so good and devout a man ..."

"I had hoped", said poor Mr Bisset, "you might have been our supply." Then, seeing that the other did not understand, he explained to him how they were without a preacher for the morrow.

The stranger spread his hands and shook his head. "But I am on holiday, sir. I have taken time off from my engrossing labours ..."

"But you are a preacher?"

— A notable preacher, if only his memory would clear: who was he? Ah! By some happy chance it came back into Mr Bisset's head. He had indeed seen this man before, though he had been too humble to speak with him: he was on the dais at the General Assembly some years before. "You are the Rev. James Rolland!" he cried.

His visitor bowed, smiling.

"Ah, I hope, sir, we shall have the privilege of sitting under you! How glad we should be, my wife and I, if you would stay under our roof; then you could conduct our service tomorrow."

As the stranger slightly frowned, Mr Bisset went eagerly on. "I trust you do not take it amiss that I ask so renowned a man? Indeed, a worse preacher would have done, only I do not know where to find one."

The other laughed, in a gentle well-bred way. "You mistake me, sir. I meant I was not worthy to fill his shoes."

At this Mr Bisset remembered that the Rev. Mr Rolland was renowned not only for eloquent preaching but also for exceptional modesty. "I do assure you, Mr Rolland," he said the more earnestly, "we should take it very kindly indeed if you were to see your way. Not only would you be doing our church an honour but you would also be taking me out of a great difficulty."

"Then I will do my best," said his visitor, half-sighing. Mr Bisset wrung him by the hand.

Tea in the drawing-room that afternoon was a pleasant affair. The ladies were captivated by their guest. They would have been somewhat in awe of him had he not made himself so approachable. He praised the teacake in a manner which commended him both to his hostess and to her cook. Indeed, he did more than praise: he ate heartily of it. He insisted upon holding her skein of wool for Grandmother. And the children's nurse flushed rosy red when in converse he deferred to her with as much respect as to Mrs Bisset herself. Though showing a liveliness in discourse, he maintained a restraint, graciously allowing others to develop topics while himself remaining silently attentive.

The children were permitted to attend, and each were presented to him: Alison, Colin and Jean. He was more affable with them even than with the grown-ups. In a moment they were at their ease. Colin pulled out and examined his gold fob-watch, which had a monogram upon it too intricate to read. Alison and Jean sat each upon one of his knees. He dandled and teased them till they were laughing. Their mother was touched.

"You are fond of little ones, Mr Rolland?"

"I dote on them, ma'am."

"You have, perhaps, a family of your own?"

She regretted the question when he lifted a sober face from between the shining heads. "Alas, no. My wife and I have not been ..."

It endeared him the more.

When the older folk went to their several duties their visitor begged to be allowed to stay in the drawing-room with the children. Their nurse went off gratefully to overtake the ironing.

The young folk got on better than ever with their new friend. They had him down on the floor, the way they did with Papa when he was in an unusually genial mood. Alison pulled off her sash and harnessed him, while little Jean clambered upon his back. He gambolled over the carpet with her, Colin getting down on his hands and knees too and gambolling at his side. Back and forward they raced with growing excitement.

"Come on, Lightfoot! Come on, Diamond! Diamond is the winner!" the Rev. Mr Rolland cried. The children were delighted with his gaiety and with his readiness in finding names for imaginary horses. Their shouts and laughter grew to such a pitch as to be scarcely consistent with the approach of Sabbath. Nurse was alarmed, and came into the drawing-room. "Children! Get up at once! How can you treat Mr Rolland in this way?"

The children begged to be allowed to go to their reverend friend at bed-time for their Bible story. They sat on the hearthrug, leaning against his knees. Colin, at their friend's request, rehearsed the story he had had the previous night from Mamma, Abraham and his mysterious journey.

"How I should love to go on a journey!" Alison sighed. "Have you ever been on a journey, sir? To far lands?"

Mr Rolland replied that he had, to Ireland and to Arabia, and even to Australia, where he had spent a number of years.

"Did you bring treasures home? For our papa has been to Africa and to Spain, and he brought back an ivory comb for Grandmamma, and a necklace of gold beads for Mamma. And he brought a Spanish doll each for Jean and me, and a bullfighter's costume for Colin."

"Nothing for himself?" asked Mr Rolland, laughing. "Poor Papa! No treasures for him?"

"O but yes!" Colin cried. "He has a collection of ancient coins, some of which he thinks are of gold. And he has a tiny statue that is of pure silver, and ... "

"Papa has many treasures," Jean said. "Papa is very rich."

"Would you like to see some of Papa's treasures?" Colin asked then. "I know where they are kept — they're in the study. I could get Papa's keys and show you. But maybe I should ask Papa first."

"I beg you will not!" their friend said. "Your papa is far too busy to think of that at present."

On the Sabbath morning their guest was so quiet that Mrs Bisset regretted she had not suggested his breakfasting alone in his bedroom. He must order his thoughts before going to church. The least she could do now was to usher him into her husband's study, make up the fire and leave him by himself.

At a quarter past ten she thought she should send to ask if he would take anything, coffee or tea or soup. The maids were busy preparing the cold luncheon of which all partook of a Sabbath. She therefore summoned Alison and entrusted her with the errand. It was Colin who knocked, softly out of respect, and waited for permission to enter. No permission was given. Was Mr Rolland in thought? In prayer? They did not know how to proceed. But there was not entire silence within. There was a slight creaking as of floorboards trodden upon. Perhaps their reverend friend was looking up one of Papa's books?

Jean in her simplicity put her eye to the keyhole. Mr Rolland was not at the bookcase, she said; he was seated at Papa's desk and he was pulling out one drawer after another. He must be looking for pen or paper? The children opened the door and went in.

Mr Rolland got quite a surprise. He thrust the drawers in and turned round. Seeing it was the children, he smiled, and to their questions answered that he had indeed been looking for a pen. "And, to tell you the truth," he went on, laughing, "your papa's desk is so amazingly like my own that I forgot for the moment where I was and felt quite confused when I did not find pens in their accustomed drawer."

Colin found him a new pen. Jean was all for sitting upon his knee and helping sort out the variety of Papa's things which were lying on top of the desk.

"But these are not Papa's best treasures!" Colin cried. "Those are in the lower drawers, the locked ones."

Mamma came bustling in. "Children! Children, come away! How can you worry Mr Rolland so near to service time?"

"I like Mr Rolland much better than Mr Chisholm," Alison remarked, while Colin edified his mother by declaring, "I know now what I want to be when I'm grown — a minister, just like Mr Rolland."

The servants and the children set off walking to church. The ladies and their guest filled the carriage, Nurse being driver. Mr Bisset himself had his horse led round to the door in order to ride at the side of the carriage.

Mr Rolland had been silent, giving a half smile when he met another's eye but not seeking converse, a mode of behaviour which all felt became him at such a time. But when he saw the horse he cried out, "Ah, what a beauty!" Mr Bisset was greatly pleased, and made his sleek brown cob show his paces a moment or two. Mr Rolland was lost in admiration. Holding on to the side of the carriage, he leant out to gaze, eagerly asking what his age might be? How many hands? By whom and out of whom?

Mr Bisset replied even more eagerly — before a cough from his lady silenced him.

They were halfway to the church; already could be seen the spire and the pointed window and the churchyard wall. They rode on a few yards in silence.

Then suddenly Mr Rolland exclaimed aloud, smiting his hand upon his coat pocket. "My notes! I have forgotten my sermon notes!"

Nurse pulled in the horse. Mr Bisset halted his cob alongside.

Mrs Bisset timidly suggested that Mr Rolland must surely not need notes? He must be well able to preach extempore. She came of a family with strict views on the matter.

But the reverend gentleman mournfully shook his head. "Alas, dear madam! Since a certain unfortunate accident when I slipped on the pulpit stairs, my memory is not of the best. It is imperative for me to have notes, the merest jotting, less for use than for the confidence it gives."

Mrs Bisset then cried, "You must certainly have them! My dear, you will ride home and fetch Mr Rolland's notes for him?"

Mr Bisset had already turned his horse.

But Mr Rolland protested vigorously. "No, sir, I beg of you! I would not put you to trouble for my trespass. Besides you are session clerk, and must go before to prepare our way. It will be far better that I should take your horse and return home." Mr Bisset demurred, but his guest prevailed. "If you will kindly give me your keys — to tell the truth, I do not exactly recall where I set them down."

He alighted from the carriage, took the keys and the reins and swung himself into the saddle, bowing to the ladies before riding back home.

"I have a surprise for you!" Mr Bisset said to his fellow elders when, themselves a little doubtful as to supply, they met him at the church door. "We are honoured to have as our preacher today the renowned Mr Rolland: The Rev. James Rolland. If you do not know who he is," he said to any who looked uncomprehending, "you will soon find out for yourselves. I feel myself fortunate to have been the means of drawing such a one into our midst."

When they asked where Mr Rolland was, he explained the

circumstances which delayed him. The elders then went in to apprise the people of the honour to be done them, while Mr Bisset bade the church officer warm the Rev. Mr Chisholm's robes before the fire, going himself to wait at the outer door.

It was the increasing volume of coughing from the congregation which confirmed Mr Bisset in his opinion that Mr Rolland was taking a long time. Had he failed to work the key in the door lock? Had he been unable to lay hands on his notes? Had the cob cast a shoe? What was keeping him?

A fidgety elder came. "Mr Bisset, time is getting on. Will you not begin the service yourself and let Mr Rolland continue when he comes? I will wait here for him to relieve you."

Alas for his expectations! Mr Bisset had to conduct the whole service himself, perforce making his prayers extempore — which should have pleased his wife at least, and giving as the sermon simply a brief account of the meeting which their absent minister was attending. He might have been excused, poor man, for being brief; the wonder was if he were coherent with it.

For he was not past announcing the second psalm when a devastating sight met his gaze through the clear glass of the window: a horseman riding swiftly out of town. It seemed beyond reasonable doubt to be the Rev. Mr Rolland on the brown cob.

The consternation of the congregation was small compared with that of the Bisset family when they arrived home. The drawers of the study desk had been swept clean of anything of value in them. Mrs Bisset's jewelbox had been ransacked too. The forks and spoons were gone from the luncheon table, the silver salvers from the sideboard. But perhaps the sorest loss of all was that of the cob.

When the Rev. Mr Chisholm arrived home from his meeting in Edinburgh, his talk was all of a scandalous affair discussed by fathers and brethren. A rogue of a horse-thief had been going around impersonating the Rev. Mr Rolland, to whom he bore a remarkable physical likeness, especially when dressed like him in a dark grey coat.

It afforded Mr Bisset small comfort that he was able to cap the tale.

Maggie the Shoppie

YOU WENT DOWN a step into Macarthurs' shoppie, and as simultaneously you opened the door a bell rang. "Ting!" This brought from the house part of the building either Mrs Macarthur or her daughter, and she served you, leaning down across the counter to see you properly. The swiftness of the response, the mystery of the sudden appearance, might make you think she had whisked in from fairyland.

If, however, you should be left for a moment or two waiting alone, you would not weary. For surely there was enough of compelling interest to make you forget the passage of time. Macarthurs' sold biscuits and jam and matches and custard powder, and fruit — if you could call some rather dry and elderly oranges by that name. They must have at some time sold cigarettes, for an advertisement composed of large letters was set out on the windowpane, on sunny days to throw long shadows on the floor. They may also have sold stout, though I never saw any trace of it. Paraffin I think they must have kept, for always the air of the shoppie smelt of it. — But what we children were interested in, what we came for, was the sweets.

There were a number of the usual impressive glass bottles, holding this and that in the way of boilings or caramels. What we loved more, however, were the individual creations; these were displayed in their several boxes on the counter which faced you as you came in at the door.

Ah, the magic of it! There were liquorice straps, ridged so that when practising economy you might tear off strips along the length, thus producing the illusion that you could eat your cake and have it. There were the two liquorice and sherbet partnerships, the sherbet

Maggie the Shoppie

sucker and the sherbet dab. The latter was a little vulgar, though very comfortable: you inserted your liquorice lozenge into the bag of sherbet, took it out, licked it, and inserted it again. The sucker was more refined, in that it did not involve your friends in an enforced inspection of your mouth: you merely sucked with dignified closed lips through the liquorice pipe. There were jelly babies, in yellow, red and black: vaguely horrifying, suggestive of Herod, but appealing in certain moods. And there were sugar mice, pink or white, with string tails, and eyes that could be so realistic that a sensitive person might shrink from taking the first bite.

When your bell had brought Mrs Macarthur, she would serve you kindly enough. "Three ha'pennies worth of jelly babies please," you would say, and she would dole them out into your sticky palm, saying, "Thank you, my dearie." If she had two or three small customers together she would have long enough for a word or two of polite inquiry. "How's all at the school the day then?" or "Are your mother's hens laying? — Tell her I was asking for her." Only her manner — she was often in a hurry, or else was apt to sigh deeply from no known cause — her manner did not invite confidences. And she might even get a little cross if one after the other we thumped down into her shop — step down, ting! — to give our small but important orders separately. "Mercy on us, bairns! Do you think I have the time to be running in and out here like the pendulum of a clock? See and be asking all you're wanting, like good bairnies now, at the same time."

Fair enough, and we did not mind. She seemed to have other preoccupations, unseen and unguessed at, in the house behind. I daresay keeping hens was one of them, and growing vegetables another; for now and then there would be a dozen eggs laid out on a high shelf above risk of breakage, or a bunch of carrots or a cabbage, looking forlorn with so little company.

Occasionally I was sent to the shoppie to buy some such dull grown-up commodity. "I must buy something from poor Mrs Macarthur," my mother would say. In a town where "poor" might mean "dear" or "nice" instead of "pitiable", I was never quite sure what was meant.

I came to the conclusion afterwards that the Macarthurs, in spite of presiding over Paradise, were quite poor. Mrs Macarthur was a sort of widow, her husband was "away". No one in Rivertown put more words to it than that, for we were in some ways a reticent people. At any rate, she was the breadwinner. I am sure she had to strain to make ends meet. She must have needed every penny and ha'penny she could bring in. But we, we said that she was mean.

For we were spoiled. We were spoiled by her daughter Maggie, Maggie the Shoppie to give her her title in full. Maggie gave the most astounding bargains. "How many bulls' eyes for a ha'penny, Maggie? Four? Aw, I thought it was five." And five it would be. — "Could I get two penny mice for three ha'pennies, Maggie?" And get them you did. — She was even known to have given a sherbet dab for nothing; that was when somebody had fallen and cut her hand. She came into the shoppie crying, and Maggie with the timely presentation dried her tears. We had so much decency in us, however, as to realise it would be taking an advantage to use tears to extract bargains. We contented ourselves with tendentious words and perhaps a wistful expression of the eyes.

Indeed, we scarcely needed any strategy at all. Maggie was on our side. She was ready to give bargains of her own accord. Unasked, she would tip the scales in our favour, shake a little more into the "poke", make two jelly babies cohere as one.

How they ever made ends meet I do not know. Maggie as a business partner must have been a liability. I think Mrs Macarthur had an idea of her ways, for we noticed that bargains were never forthcoming when she was around. It was on the joyful occasions when Maggie was alone in the shoppie that our expectations were high. Many of us, indeed, would prudently retain our money till the word had gone round, "It's Maggie in the shoppie," to buy or to receive.

But apart from the bargains, we loved when Maggie was in the shoppie. She always had time for us. And she was such fun. A jest would bring roars of laughter, or a jest in return.

"How's all at the school the day?" she would ask the stock question.

"Hoch, we're hanging the teacher."

"Do you tell me that?" she would say, shaking her head in mock solemnity. "And is that all they can learn you?" And she would flatter us with her laughter.

She was jolly; and she was very kind. I remember what must have been my first remembered meeting with Maggie. My eldest sister had taken me into the shoppie and was apologising for me, "She's awful wee, Maggie." I can still hear Maggie's voice, gentle, warm, "Aye she's wee. But she's smart, what's of her." I think her approval then did more for me than anything else since; she gave me confidence in myself.

That was the way of it with all of us. The whole air of the shoppie was full not only of paraffin but of happiness and well-being. Here you felt at ease, your spirit grew and spread, you rose to heights, you could think and say amusing things.

I remember Maggie best as this loving happy presence. Her outward appearance I remember only dimly. She is represented by a detail here and there, the way her skirt hung, the crinkles in her stout mis-shapen shoes. And I remember with curious vividness a necklace she sometimes wore, of pale mottled shells. My sister had one not unlike it; but she never wore it after she was, say, fifteen. I wondered why Maggie should wear, as a grown-up lady, what might be considered more fit for a child.

Maggie had brown eyes. — Now that I noticed on the only occasion I ever saw her clearly as a whole person.

It was a few days after a new little girl had come to our class at school. She was to stay only a few months, as a matter of fact; her parents were home on holiday from abroad. She was very rich, to judge by the chocolate biscuits she always had for "break", and the number and variety of her pairs of shoes. She was different from us in other ways. Her shining pigtails were secured up on her head with ribbons: it gave her a prim, or as we would say, old-fashioned look. She had worn her hair this way abroad, she would explain, for the heat. She would, if encouraged, describe at great length the grandeur of her life out East, the pillared verandahs, the trailing flowers, the swift obsequious servants, her parents' exalted state. We would listen gravely, never showing that her tale held us not by its interest but its oddity.

We were perhaps a little too apt to see the comic in what was different from ourselves. The only excuse I can offer is that at least we did not show the amusement we felt. Only a slight tightening of the muscle at the corner of the mouth, a small widening of the eyes, would indicate the fact that inwardly we were convulsed with laughter.

The little girl's speech, too, was different from ours, which added the final touch. It was probably simply the speech of some other part of Scotland, of England maybe: her mother, it was said, came from the South.

Her connection with Inverness was through her father. He had, apparently, been born and brought up in our town, in the very part of it, indeed, where we lived. His old home was only a few doors off from the shoppie. Now his parents, following in his financial wake, had removed to a more fashionable quarter; and it was there that the little girl and her mother and father were staying.

Well, we were all of us in the shoppie one day, for the word had gone round that it was Maggie. We were trying to decide between liquorice straps, jelly babies and the rest of them, when, ting! went the doorbell, and down into the shoppie stepped the little stranger girl and someone who seemed to be her father. The little girl stared solemnly at us, and we even more solemnly back at her. It was with the tail of my eye that I saw her father approach Maggie. He said nothing for a bit. And she said nothing either. Taken separately I suppose they would have seemed to me of immeasurable age: standing together they suddenly appeared to be at least contemporaries, almost a sort of older boy and girl. I was lost in this speculation when Maggie softly spoke, "What would you be wanting?"

He said in the same tone, "Anything, Maggie, anything."

Maggie went to one of the large glass bottles, removed the stopper, and with something more than her usual abandon poured the sweets into the bag, and gave it brimming to the man, who received it as heedlessly. For a moment they stood together again. I heard the murmur of their voices, an ordinary conversation enough. —

"And how have you all been, Maggie?"

"We should be thankful."

"You're all right yourself then?"

"I'm fine, thank you. How's all with you?"

The little girl began to pull her father's sleeve. "Come on, come on, Daddy!" He allowed himself to be pulled, but his head was turned backwards till he reached the door.

Here an unexpected scene occurred. A lady was seen to be waiting for them outside. She must have been the mother. Her speech was like the little girl's. Now she spoke, in a clear loud voice, accenting the second syllable of every sentence. "How LONG you've taken! What HAVE you been doing? Why DID you go into such a shop in any case? Such a DIRTY little shop!"

Ting! We took advantage of their being now outside to snigger openly. Lachie, the boldest of us, put on a grotesque show of elegance and said, "The Countess of Clachnacuddin, on a shopping tour!" at which we all burst out laughing together.

Maggie alone gave no sign of amusement. It drew our eyes to her.

What was the matter with her? She was standing behind the counter, gripping it with her hands so that the knuckles were white. I remember them being white, as I rememeber the skin being all bleached and wrinkled with some washing she had done, I suppose, before coming to serve in the shop. She could not surely have been offended by the lady's remark about the shoppie? That would, to us, have been less than reasonable. The lady, like the little girl, plainly belonged to the world of comedy. — Do you take offence at a monkey for making a face at you?

What was the matter then? Maggie was leaning over the counter which she was gripping with those hands, and it was then I saw that her eyes were brown, for she was gazing with them, gazing out through the window with its shadowy letters to the trio walking away up the street. I was puzzled at the look on her face. It was one neither of indignation nor of pain. It was one I had never seen before, indeed have rarely seen since: the look of passionate love.

To break the uncanny silence we began to call out our demands.

"Any mint rolls the day, Maggie? I'll take twopennies worth — my rich uncle's died."

"Maggie, will you give me a sugar mouse?"

"Have you got sherbet suckers in again yet, Maggie?"

To our surprise and concern she took no heed of us at all. Our words echoed unanswered within the shoppie. We could not believe it — our Maggie, so kind, so attentive to us, was taking no notice. She seemed not even to hear us. Gradually, with growing alarm, we realised that for her we were not there at all. She was alone in the shoppie. We did not exist.

This was a destroying thought, we could not endure it. Desperately, rudely, we bawled out in chorus. "Maggie, where's the sugar mice? The sugar mice? THE SUGAR MICE?" We thrust our faces towards hers. One of us caught up an empty box and waved it roughly in front of her fixed eyes.

Like some slow and clumsy beast then under the shouts of its herds, she turned from us and lumbered to the pile of sweetie boxes standing in loose array against the wall. She began to fumble up and down them. We watched, for the moment relieved. — Till suddenly she had thrust in her hands between the boxes to the wall, and let her head fall forward between her arms.

She couldn't be —? It wasn't possible. Did grown-ups —?

We would have given all the sugar mice in the world to be able to pull away our eyes, drawn as if by some evil spell to the still figure at the wall. An eternity of embarrassment it was. We looked in agony at last to Lachie, to see if he could say something.

"Hoch, Maggie, never heed," he did say. "If you canna find them, the world willna come to an end. We'll get them another day. — We'll have to be off now, Maggie. There's a match on."

Thankfully we followed his lead. "Never heed, never heed, Maggie. It's something else I was wanting after all. Look it's here."

"We'll take them from here, Maggie. And thanks."

"Many thanks, Maggie."

It was all we could do for her, to go away. In an effort to help further, however, we took all our pennies and ha'pennies and laid them down on the counter as noiselessly as we could, for once in our lives taking nothing in return for them. And we went out of the doorway quietly, that is, all on the same ting!

And the next time we went into the shoppie, Maggie was as jolly as ever, and giving bargains the same as before.